Book Six of The Deception Series

Prequel to Web of Deception

Workings

Of

I0598518

Deception

Ryan Hodge

SMP Publishing Edition

Printed in the United States of America

10 9 8 7 6 5 4 3 2 1

ISBN: 978-0-9977990-5-7 (PBK)

DEDICATION

My dear mother,
Thank you for being steady,
in this world filled with uncertainty,
you made sure we were ready.
Thank you for the words you said,
they still provide relevant guidance,
in days current and ahead.
Thank you for a life of showering love,
In the frostiest winter there was no cold,
warmth you gave was perfect fitting like a tailored
made glove.
Thank you for not being driven by material things,
they are nice to have, but not vital,
because you knew material love allows to be
controlled by strings.
Thank you for being brilliant,
in more ways than one,
you were radiant and extremely resilient.
My dear mother.

.

CHAPTER 1

"Alright Sage, it damn sure seems like this latest attempt on my life is retaliation for some of *your* bullshit. The man who tried to kill me implied that his beef with me was directly related to beef he had with you. I need to know what the fuck is going on. You have some serious explaining to do. This can't wait; I need to know right now and we're not parting ways until you tell me precisely what you did to that guy for him to want to kill me," Sheena verbalizes in an enraged fashion.

I respond, "I know you're concerned about what transpired, but it's really irrelevant now because it's over and the guy's dead. Whatever happened back in the day doesn't matter because it has no bearing on our lives going forward. Just trust that you, the boys, and I are all safe now. That drama died with that man tonight."

"Umm, you must be outta ya fuckin mind Sage! That shit ain't flying with me right now! I want full disclosure as to why someone wanted to get back at you so badly that he didn't just go after you. He had to have a different kinda hurt if he wanted to cause pain to your loved ones. Apparently, Mrs. Kline is a focal point to all of this, so it's time to spill the beans. All of this being secretive and incognito is out of the fucking window! I need answers now damn it! You owe the full truth to me and the boys for putting us through hell on earth," Sheena demands.

I say, "Calm down...calm down. You're right. I do owe you the truth and I'll be open and honest with you, but I'm warning you that I'm going to share everything with you including the good, the bad, and the ugly. Once I start telling you what was going on, don't tell me that you don't want to hear what I have to say. With that being said, if you still want to hear what happened, I'll continue."

"I asked you for full disclosure, so spit it out. I'm not a little ass girl and I don't need any warnings. There's nothing you can tell me that I can't handle. I'm a Jersey girl and I'm not weak in any form or fashion. Besides, my life has been on the line several times and I was able to endure that, so by no means can a story do me any harm. Tell me e-ve-ry-thing," Sheena voices.

I can tell by the look of intent in Sheena's eyes that she isn't going to let this go. She wants to know what happened that caused her life to be on the line. I totally understand her position because I would want to know what caused all of this conflict too. I ponder leaving many parts of the story out, but I decide that I'll be fully forthcoming and tell her everything. Besides, it's all old news now and nothing negative will come of it.

"Yo, there's so much to tell that I don't even know where to start," I speak.

Sheena answers promptly, "It's not that hard. Just start at the beginning of whatever got all of the drama going. That way, I'll have a clear picture of why this happened. I just wanna be able to make sense of it all."

"Okay, if the entire story is what you want, the entire story is what you shall receive. Honestly, the story starts from the very first day I got on Howard University's campus. I really mean day one," I tell.

"I'm all ears Sage," Sheena utters sternly.

I decided to start college during the second summer session instead of waiting until the fall semester. We were broke as hell in Linden, so there really wasn't much going on for me there. As you know, I was the top of my class in high school, but still hadn't chosen a major in college. An undecided major was cool with me at that point because I would only be taking general classes anyway. I hoped going to school early would help me figure out the career path for me.

Many people think having tons of options makes the decision-making process easier, but it actually complicates matters. It's like someone offering you twenty vacations and telling you to only pick one. If they are all great destinations, how do you easily choose just one? I also wanted to get on campus early because I knew finding a job would be a million times easier if I arrived before the majority of the student body got there. I had heard all of the horror stories about how many college students are dead broke in school.

My cousin, who attended college years before me would always say, "I was super broke in college. I used to eat Ramen noodles every day. Sometimes, I would only have Pop Tarts to eat. I had to really learn to stretch a dollar. Those were tough times, but well worth it."

I did not want that to be my fate. I refused to call around begging for money and struggling. My scholarships paid my tuition, but didn't leave much money to do anything else with. I knew I needed to get a job that would be flexible. I eventually found the perfect job for me and my class schedule. I got a job at a lounge named Kline's Lounge. It was my first day on campus and I remember I was riding my bike past the lounge and almost didn't stop inside to see if they were hiring because the couple who owned the spot were out in the parking lot arguing about the lounge. I said this couldn't be a good environment to work in, but then I said this may be the perfect spot for me. I pondered on it for just a minute and began riding towards the entrance. The couple concluded their argument and walked in just before I chained my bike. To my surprise, I was given an interview right then and there. The interview went well and I was hired on the spot. Mrs. Kline, who was one of the owners, was very kind and pleasant from the first time we met. She was nice enough to let me make my own schedule. The job was great for me because it was easy, allowed me to meet people, and get my classwork done while earning some bread, but there was a drawback.

The drawback was that there weren't a lot of people coming through the doors. Mr. and Mrs. Kline were an older couple and had no idea how to relate to the younger crowd, so not a lot of college kids patronized the spot. I knew that Kline's Lounge could be a popping spot because of its close proximity to Howard University's campus, but it would take some fresh ideas to draw a crowd and innovative changes to the décor to make patrons want to come back. Unfortunately, a lot of old people are stuck in their ways and don't welcome change. The Klines were the consummate example of people who were stuck in their ways. They were traditionalists to say the least. The truth is that traditional thinking does not work in this business. You have to be willing to adapt on a daily basis and keep up with the times.

I knew with some hard work and creative thinking that the lounge would be a gold mine. I figured that I should be the person to bring the new ideas to the table, but benefit from it too. It was a gamble, but it really didn't matter because it would only be a matter of time before the place would have to shut down if they didn't get more business. The best part of the gamble was that it wouldn't cost me any cash if it didn't work. I told Mr. and Mrs. Kline that I wanted to have a meeting with them to discuss some business with the lounge. Unfortunately, Mr. Kline refused to sit down with me because he really wanted to be out of the lounge business anyway. He was old and frail and wasn't as sharp as he once was. However, Mrs. Kline accepted my offer to have a sit down. We sat at a booth in the lounge while we conversed.

"Sage, what do you want to discuss about the lounge?" Mrs. Kline inquired.

"Well, I want to start off by saying that you have a very lovely establishment here and I don't mean to slight it while we're conversing," I said.

Mrs. Kline replied, "Thank you, young man. I love this place and have many memories associated with it. My husband and I didn't always own this place. We actually met at this same lounge when we were in college attending Howard University. We came here frequently when we were students. Ultimately, that is the reason why we purchased it. I hope you don't intend to insult this place that I love so much."

"That's special Mrs. Kline and I'm sure there are millions of family memories here, but you know like I do, that they may come to an abrupt end if more people don't walk through those doors. Frankly, the place is dull and that's why people don't come here in high volumes," I verbalized.

She answered as her voice quivered, "Sage, I know. It actually saddens me when I think about losing this place. It has been a part of our family for forever. In fact, I used to feed my daughter Jasmine at this very table."

I spoke, "I couldn't imagine the possibility of losing something dear to me. The good thing is that maybe you don't have to lose it. I want to try to turn this place around with your permission. We can make it a business deal for the both of us."

"That sounds fantastic Sage! What do you have in mind?" Mrs. Kline asked enthusiastically.

I told her that I planned to increase the traffic coming through the lounge exponentially. I explained to her that if I was able to increase profits the lounge that I would want to keep a small percentage of the increase. Basically, once they made the amount of money they would generally make each month, I would get a percentage of everything thereafter. Mrs. Kline liked the idea of what I suggested because there was no way she could lose. If the lounge didn't profit any from my actions, then she wouldn't have to pay. If the lounge did profit more than normal, then I would get paid for my services.

"I know you have to run it by Mr. Kline first, so just let me know," I voiced.

She uttered, "Mr. Kline doesn't concern himself with the business of the lounge too much these days. I can give you an answer now if you like."

"The sooner the better," I answered.

"My answer is that we have a deal. If you can turn this place around, I'm all for the deal you proposed," Mrs. Kline told me.

"Great! This is a fantastic day to say the least! Mrs. Kline I won't let you down. However, I do have one immediate suggestion," I vocalized."

Mrs. Kline articulated, "I trust you'll turn this place. Tell me about this immediate suggestion you have."

"Thanks for your confidence. As far as the immediate suggestion is concerned I think it's time for a name change," I replied.

Mrs. Kline responded, "I'm open to a name change. Something tells me that you already have something in mind."

I chuckled and said, "I certainly do. The new name should be In the Mix."

"That's very catchy Sage! I love it! I'll start the process of changing the name," Mrs. Kline words.

I was extremely excited about my new business

venture that cost me nothing upfront, but put me in a position to make plenty of cash. I knew I'd be making a lot of money, but I also knew it would take a lot of work. However, it didn't matter because I was prepared for it. I had only been in D.C. for a month and was already making moves. Mrs. Kline and I worked out the specifics of the agreement. She was all business and even typed up the contract stating the specifics of our deal and we both signed it. Mrs. Kline even went as far to have a couple of customers serve as witnesses to the agreement. All I had to do was make it happen.

I was always good at strategizing, so I used my natural abilities to my benefit. I made as many friends on campus as humanly possible and invited them to the lounge. I also printed up hundreds of flyers and placed them wherever I could around campus and the city. I promoted the lounge so much that I think I even had advertisements on the moon. In some instances, I would tell girls on campus that I'd buy their first drink if they came to the lounge and post pictures to their social media accounts. I knew the money would eventually come back to me, so I saw it as an investment.

I knew we'd need a DJ for the lounge and Howard University had a lot of aspiring DJs, so I propositioned them. Since they were not the least bit known, I was able to get them to DJ in the lounge for free. I had four DJs in total to work the four days of the week that I needed DJs. Also, I hired fraternity members to provide security for the lounge because they didn't want much money and I knew frat members carried a large constituency.

The fall semester was starting soon, so I knew that students would want to have a place to party and In the Mix had to be the place they'd come. By default, there are more people in town who want to party, so naturally the lounge would have more profits, which meant that I'd get my cut of the profits. Also, I knew the lounge would directly benefit from a policy that Howard University had. The policy stated that freshman students couldn't have cars. In the Mix was within walking distance of Howard's campus and dorms, so most freshman would be inclined to walk over to the lounge to chill.

Luckily, everything I thought would happen actually did. The fall semester started and the students started pouring in. Once Thursday hit, the people coming to the lounge were nonstop until Sunday. Mrs. Kline didn't really stick around for too much of the lounge's nightlife because it just was too boisterous for her. She would come to the lounge during the early hours of the day to make sure things behind the scenes were copacetic. She was happy about how things were going and always joked with me about the money I was making from being so good at what I did.

Mrs. Kline said on many instances, "You are making more money off tips than I am making off alcohol and food. Your personality is perfect for this job. I always hear you passing off advice to the customers. They seem to really appreciate it. This place has really started seeing more business since you've been around."

It seemed like every time I turned around, I was being asked for answers to different questions and scenarios. It was through my job at the lounge that I figured out what I wanted to major in at school. I decided to double major in Counseling Psychology and Business. I hoped that this career path would allow me to hone my skills in assisting people with their problems. It became an easy choice and I was convinced that this would be my dream job.

The classes I took to meet the requirements for my major were a breeze. They were always interesting and I was always excited to go to class. I took what I learned in class and immediately implemented those strategies in helping customers at the lounge. I was at Kline's Lounge so much that it became a second home for me. It was an ideal place to be because although I worked there, I really enjoyed being there. Additionally, there were a couple of rooms in the back of the lounge and one of them was mine. I had more of my belongings in my room at the lounge than I did in my dorm room. It would be nothing for me to go days without stopping by my dorm. If my roommates wanted to see me, they, along with everyone else, would hit the lounge. Dave is my older brother and was my roommate during my freshmen year in college. He would say, "You look like my lil brother, but I am not 100% sure because I don't see him anymore. Don't work too hard lil bruh. You don't want to miss out on all of these females here at school. You know they outnumber us seven to one on campus."

That was typical of my brother. He had an unquenchable thirst for women. He would meet women at the lounge and before you know it, they were leaving his bedroom in the middle of the night or the next morning. He had girls from everywhere and every race too. He didn't care if they found out about each other either. One night he purposely scheduled two females to come to the lounge at the same time. He wanted to talk himself into a threesome with the two ladies. I think it played out better in his head because both females were extremely upset. They ended up having a huge altercation.

Shells, was one of the girls who was arguing that night. We nicknamed her "Shells" because she was from Myrtle Beach, South Carolina and the other girl was Deena. She was from Phoenix, Arizona.

"You don't want none of this! This ain't nothing to play with bitch," Deena said.

Shells replied, "You will get cut the fuck up in

this lobby. I told you to take your ass on!"

Next thing you know, Shells and Deena were fighting through the lobby. They broke the glass table that was nicely placed along the wall for decor. The sound of the crash of the table breaking was like two trucks carrying glass bottles colliding head on while doing seventy miles per hour. Shells grabbed ahold of Deena's hair and yanked her down the hall. Deena eventually fell to the floor and after a brief tussle, Shells began pounding Deena's head repeatedly into the floor. Blood was everywhere. Most of the lounge patrons were in the lobby watching by then. By the time the lounge security was able to separate them, both girls were out of breath, bloody, and half dressed. They both got a free ride to the county jail that night. Later, we found out that Deena had a concussion from all of the head jerking and bashing into the floor.

Dave said, "They messed up my night. Fighting for no reason. They coulda both been with me and had a great night. Instead, I gotta get somebody else to come over. No damn sense. I coulda bust both of them bitches down."

Dave's response shocked many people who overheard it, but not me though. Dave had that same mentality about women for his entire adult life. He refused to put them before him because he had been played by his high school sweetheart. Ever since then, he did not care about chicks or how they felt, but that's a story of its own.

"From now on, me first and all else second," uttered Dave one day after his former girlfriend betrayed his trust.

He certainly lived it. Dave didn't finish college. He focused too much on the girls and not enough on his studies. It seemed like he only went to college to have sex and do women dirty. He eventually resigned from school and took his drama back to our hometown in Linden.

The lounge was a success and so was I. There was a big disparity between what I made in tips and what the other bartenders made. It would be nothing for me to get a hundred dollar tip or in many instances even more. People liked the fact that I took time to help them with their problems. I met countless people from all walks of life. I should have known that I'd become a success with the ladies too, but I was being naïve.

There were some drawbacks to working at the lounge. Obviously, people got into altercations there, but that was to be expected. Another negative thing about the lounge was there were always fake ballers and pretenders in there. These were the people who wanted everyone to think a certain way about them, but really they were the opposite. They were people who were putting on fronts for everyone in the spot. Clearly, they were trying to hide their shortcomings and insecurities in life. Another thing I did not enjoy was the way dudes were constantly "running game" on the females who came through the club. "Running game" is a form of manipulation dudes use on females to get what they want from them. Most of the time, the woman is left hurt, empty, and alone, while the dude is laughing with his boys about what he thinks he has accomplished. It really bothered me how men put so much effort into playing women for sex. Many of these guys did not have any goals as far as careers were concerned. They really felt like scoring for the night was the best thing in the world. It baffled me how they could not see that sex is only a minor part of relationships and life. Some of these guys were very smart, but did not maximize their aptitude. If they focused on more fruitful endeavors, they could own their own businesses or at a minimum be the president of a fortune 500 company. Instead of using their mental savvy to advance their position in life, they did nothing with it, but party and run the streets. I remember me and Mrs. Kline had a conversation about how they were wasting their time jumping from club to club.

"You have to remember a few things about people and life. Everyone has different goals in life and their goals are not for you to criticize. Another thing is that you only have to focus on your life. Life, liberty, and the pursuit of happiness. That was written because each person is free to live life the way they choose. If you judge what they do with their lives, they can surely judge you too. Someone who doesn't approve of bartending can surely cast a stone at you. The fact they don't approve doesn't make them right," she said.

I knew she was right, but I had a plan for my future. Those guys were just living day to day with no idea of what their future would be like. I did not go back and forth with her.

"I had not thought of it that way. Thank you for the wise words," I replied.

"Besides that, Sage, if the guys you speak so negatively about stop coming through my doors, we'll both be out of a job and at the unemployment building downtown. Remember this - no guys in here, equals no girls in here. Which turns into no money in here," she quickly replied.

We both laughed uncontrollably as we set up the lounge for the day's customers. As the days breezed by, the lounge grew in popularity. It was almost like the lounge and I were growing together because my popularity was soaring around town too. The lounge over the year had seen a mix of clientele. The college crowd frequented the place as well as people who wanted to host parties such as bridal showers and sweet sixteens. Famous athletes and other professional people who made a lot of money patronized the lounge too. Needless to say, I was able to save a great deal of money from the extra services I provided at the lounge. In the Mix and me were forever linked as one.

One night, a middle-aged woman, who was a regular customer, came in alone and sat down. I immediately knew something was wrong because she never came in alone. She was always with a group of friends or family members. Not to mention, her facial expression was nothing close to happy. Her face was so hot with anger she could have started a forest fire. Unfortunately, her facial expression was one that I had seen many times during my childhood.

Sadly, I've seen my share of heartbreak on the faces of the women who were closest to me. They were victims of scandalous men who sought to hurt their feelings and mislead them. They would make women think they were serious about them, but all the time were just plotting instead. Some were scheming for sex, while others were scheming for money. Whatever their motives were, it was totally wrong and uncalled for. I knew I had to help my good customer Maggie get through this tough time.

I said, "Mag, how are you?"

In a very low and sullen voice she said, "I have been better."

I replied, "Can I fix you a drink? What seems to be the trouble?"

She replied, "You know my favorite. I'll have one of them. I am having a tumultuous time in my relationship right now and I don't know what's going on."

I asked, "What is your man doing or not

doing?"

"Well, I do not know what to think. It started out with him being in his phone a lot. He would claim he was surfing the web, but it always appeared he was texting. A lot of times his phone would ring, but he wouldn't answer it. Plus, he would never let me use his phone, not even for a minute. I don't consider myself to be insecure, but I really think something is going on," she stated.

I asked, "Did you ask him about his actions in a non-threatening way?"

She replied, "Yes, I did, but he blew it off. He made it seem like I had no reason to feel the way I felt. We've had several conversations like this, but my point never seemed to get through. Finally, out of the blue, he began volunteering his phone to me. He would even leave it out unattended. That was extremely uncanny because he always took his phone with him throughout the day."

I asked, "Out of the blue he just switched it up, huh?"

I knew that the chances of him changing that drastically were very slim. He started out always using his phone and protecting it every chance he got to barely using it and often leaving it unattended. I explained to her that it is possible that he changed for the better and that her words finally clicked in his head, but it is unlikely. I told her he most likely found a solution to the problem. He needed to get her off his back, so he probably purchased another phone that she didn't know about. This would allow him to freely send messages to whoever he wanted to without worrying about her finding out. He could relieve himself of having to erase messages from the phone and wouldn't have to worry about Mag going on the internet and looking up his phone records.

What her guy was running on her is called the "Active Cover Up". This is a strategy men use to get over on women. Deception is used as a tool to subdue the woman's suspicions. He allows her to use his phone to deceive her into thinking he's on the up and up. It is really an attempt to cover up the mistakes he has made in his shifty dealings. In this instance, the other phone provided him cover to cheat on his lady. He was no longer using his phone at a high rate, so she would let her guard down.

After I told her what I thought, she told another very interesting story. She told me that she called him one night and he stated he was in bed about to fall asleep. She further explained that during their conversation she heard a phone ring. He claimed it was his house phone, but she didn't believe that with certainty because it was a ring she never heard before.

"Be confident in what you know. It may be worth your time to investigate a little bit and see if you can find some proof to support your suspicions. Don't think you are crazy," I told her.

She thanked me for the insight and comforting words, then finished her drink and left me two crisp one hundred dollar bills. The bills were so crisp that I got a paper cut when I picked them up. Receiving huge tips for a few minutes of my time happened so frequently that I wasn't even surprised anymore. I opened a savings account to keep the tip money I earned. I never spent a single penny of it either. I watched the money grow over the years. It took everything in me to not go buy a brand new car or line my closet with expensive clothes. I didn't because I knew I had bigger goals to accomplish. I would not be deterred in reaching my goal. It would take mental fortitude, but I was fully confident that I would stick to my plan.

In the Mix was the consummate name change for Kline's Lounge. It was perfect because it really captured the essence of how I felt. There was always something going on at the place. I was completely engulfed in all the daily and nightly happenings even when they were seemingly simple.

One night, a regular patron named Kim came to the lounge for an outing with her friends. She arrived well before her friends, so she sat at the bar until they arrived. While she was sitting at the bar, another customer saw her sitting there alone and motioned me over to him.

"What's up man? Is the lady at the bar with

anybody? She is fly," he commented.

"Nah, she is alone for now. She is meeting up with some friends soon though. Better make a swift move," I replied.

"Send her a drink on me. Whatever she's drinking. Then let her know I sent it," he requested.

I did as the gentleman asked and fixed her a drink of her choice. She happily accepted the drink and before you know it, the guy was sitting next to her. They had a long conversation about various topics. I couldn't help from overhearing because I was setting things up and they even asked my opinion on a few of the topics. Eventually, she gave the guy her number and he left a few minutes before her friends arrived.

She said, "He seemed like a really nice guy. That was very sweet of him to buy me a drink. We need more nice guys like that in the world. What did you think of him?"

"That's really not for me to decide. He approached you, not me," I told her.

"Come on. I want your honest opinion of him. He seems real goal oriented and driven. I love a determined man," she remarked.

I said, "Seemed is the optimal word in your statement. You can't make that determination off of one short conversation."

"Are you saying he is not hard working and determined? It seemed like it to me," she stated.

"Honestly, that guy runs the same game over

and over. It's dry and over done," I told her.

"What game is that?" she asked emphatically.

"That guy does not work nearly as much as he is letting on. He is pulling the wool over your eyes," I said.

When her eyes lit up, I knew I had her attention. The look in her eyes asked me the question before her mouth could utter the things she wanted to know. I explained to her that he is setting her up. What he did was make his "Proposal". Not a proposal as used when pertaining to marriage, but in a different denotation of the word. A proposal is also a plan or a scheme. I told her about how he uses this "Proposal" to start his manipulative process. For example, she just met him and has already accepted that he works often. He will use this to his advantage. He's going to wine and dine her upfront because his schedule has been relaxed lately then he will eventually become too busy and unavailable. She'll be accepting of his sudden business because he has already told her his situation. During their initial meeting, he made a proposal to her. She can either accept the proposal or not. His hope is that she proceeds in dealing with him. The timing of the "Proposal" is key to its success. The proposal will be offered up during the first meeting or very early in the dating process. There are two reasons why the timing is important. One reason is a woman is more likely to believe him if the "Proposal" is given sooner than later. Another reason why an early proposal is necessary is because it is less suspicious if he presents the "Proposal" when he supposedly has no reason to lie. He does not know the female and she doesn't know him, so it seems unnecessary for him to lie. The dude also uses the "Proposal" to cover his many clandestine relationships with women. He will always be able to use his busy schedule as a cover when he can't make dates or other outings that may be planned. The most ideal part of the "Proposal" is that the accepting party really can't get mad at him because he was straight forward about his fluctuating schedule. If the female decides to stop talking to him, he probably won't care because by then he has probably already had sex with his target. The lady was dumbfounded by what I told her.

I started to feel like the lounge was my child and I was charged with raising and protecting it. I had to nurture the venue to ensure it was a success. Any drama that occurred, I had to extinguish it. I thoroughly enjoyed the challenge of trying to find diplomatic solutions to the disagreements people had. I didn't want to take anything from Mrs. Kline because she was a great owner, but she was up in age and did not have the energy I had to invest in the lounge.

"I will handle all of the heavy lifting around here Mrs. Kline. You are the brains and I am the brawn of the operation. That's what works for us, we have a great relationship. If anything happens that we need muscles for, I am your guy," I said all the time.

She definitely had all of the knowhow and business savvy to run the place. I learned a lot from Mrs. Kline through the years I worked there. Without her tutelage, I don't think I would have the success that I had bartending. Not only that, Mrs. Kline taught me a lot about life. She taught me things that transferred to all facets of life.

CHAPTER 2

"Sheena, I was doing my thing at da lounge. I still remember when I was named staff supervisor," I say.

Mrs. Kline voiced, "Sage you're doing an awesome job here at the lounge. You're such a valuable asset to the staff. You're also a true leader. You found a way to unite the employees and minimize differences between them. I am going to promote you to the staff supervisor. You have such a great rapport with our customers. They seem to come just to talk to you sometimes. Not only do you help the staff with their problems, you also solve the problems that many of our customers have. I think you deserve a raise. The lounge has been able to cut back on expenses since you joined our staff. Some of your ideas have really helped us shave our overhead. I have been tracking our monthly earning trends since shortly after your employment with us and we have aggrandized our profits each quarter. I hope you don't leave our team, but I know that it is inevitable. Sage, I know you have a mission for your future and will not be denied or deterred. I respect you for that. I wish more young men were like you. I know you will be successful in your future endeavors. You being here allowed me to not work as hard and gave me the necessary time to heal from the hardships of my divorce. Not only that, my stress level and blood pressure are down because I don't have to worry about the lounge like I used to. Knowing you're on the job affords me the opportunity to have peace of mind and for that I'm indebted to you."

I graciously responded, "Mrs. Kline, that truly means a lot to me. I can't thank you enough for hiring me. You took a chance on me when you didn't have to and it all worked out. Your tutelage has enabled me to have the success that I've had. I couldn't have done it without you! Thank you for the opportunity; I won't let you down."

"I guess we've helped each other. That's the way business is supposed to go. We're supposed to help one another reach our goals. I look forward to many more years of collaboration," Mrs. Kline replied.

"I do too Mrs. Kline! Thanks for sticking around tonight. It's a big night for the lounge and we can use your help," I spoke.

She answered, "No problem!"

It was Halloween, so I asked Mrs. Kline to schedule all of In the Mix's employees to work. Halloween has always been one of our busiest nights of the year since I've been around. People seem to love to be out and about for Halloween. In addition to it being Halloween, it also happened to be a Saturday too. That year we threw a huge costume party at the lounge to celebrate. One year, a girl showed up as Wonder Woman. Her outfit was so skimpy and tight that you could see everything she had to offer. It definitely did not leave anything for the guys to wonder about. If anything, they only wondered how they could take her home for the night.

Another costume that made many of the guys take a double and triple look was seemingly not a costume. The woman had on a men's dress shirt and some high heeled shoes. All of the dudes wondered what the outfit was a costume at all. It was clear to me what her outfit represented.

A random dude said, "Excuse me sweetheart. I do not mean any disrespect, but why didn't you wear a costume? Or is it?"

"I am wearing a costume. Can't you tell? I wouldn't have this on just for no reason," she replied.

"I figured it was, but asked to be certain. I didn't want to think it was a costume if it wasn't. In that case, I have no idea what your costume is then," said the man.

She replied, "My costume is really not complicated. In fact, it's quite simple. It is called the morning after... You know, like the morning after sex. Women sometimes will put on the dude's shirt that she had sex with while she walks around the house."

"Oh ok, I get it now! That is pretty clever of you. I know that I've never seen that costume before," uttered the man. "If it's truly the night after costume, you shouldn't be wearing any panties, thong, or anything."

"I know how to fully complete a costume when I wear one. I'm not slack. And no, I am not wearing any undergarments," she retorted as she walked away from the man.

That happened the first Halloween I was at the lounge. Halloween always made for a wild and interesting night at the lounge. The crazies come out on Halloween for sure. Many like to use it as an excuse to be free and do whatever their wild side desires. The lounge was packed on Halloween the previous year and that night was no different. The line was wrapped around the building and was two people wide. I saw the thirst and the excitement in the eyes of people waiting to get inside. They were thirsty for the excitement that Halloween brings and they were thirsty for adult beverages and adult activities. The security guards were working extra hard that night because they had to frisk everyone who wanted to enter the lounge. They had double the people to search on a night like that night. I have to admit, I was a little excited myself. I normally made a bundle of extra cash from the tips the Halloween crowd brought. We charged an extra dollar per drink on Halloween night and the staff got to split all that extra money between them. This was an idea I ran past Mrs. Kline a couple of years prior. I figured since we all worked extra hard on nights like Halloween, that we should be compensated for it. She was in favor of it because was the right thing to do and no additional money came out of her pockets. Dealing with her was always pleasant. Mrs. Kline was very diplomatic and almost ran the lounge like a democracy. She was always open to new innovative ideas. Anything that kept the peace and benefitted the club, she was down for. I was glad she had the controlling percentage of the lounge. Mrs. Kline held the majority ownership, while her ex-husband and daughter held minority ownership percentages.

The few times I interacted with Mr. Kline were always brief, but severely unpleasant. He was a bitter older gentleman who was angry at the world. The staff members and I always called him the Black Mr. Scrooge behind his back. Even though he couldn't fire us, we still respected him because of Mrs. Kline. He was also a bit of a hypocrite. I remember overhearing a conversation between him and Mrs. Kline.

"I don't want anything to do with these clubs, lounges, and bars. They are beneath me. We need to invest in something more prestigious and less work like a hotel. They pretty much run themselves. The parent company takes care of all of the advertising," he screamed.

Mrs. Kline replied, "I don't see why we would sell something that we started together and it's profitable. We do not know what might happen with a hotel. It could flop."

He articulated, "Bars come and go all the time. Hotels on the other hand, hotels stay around for generations. The lounge could be shut down in the blink of an eye. All it would take is for somebody to get hurt or an underage kid to sneak in and have a drink. The city officials will have boards on the windows faster than you can say shut down."

Mrs. Kline stated simply, "I am not planning for any of that to happen. In the Mix is here to stay."

That was their relationship. They argued almost every time they were in the company of one another. They were married for many years until things went south. Mr. Kline hated the lounge, but I think he hated it more because it was the love of Mrs. Kline's life. She probably liked it more than she liked her husband when they were together. Mr. Kline always said the nightlife business wasn't for him and he wanted no parts of it, but he surely enjoyed the check he got every month from its earnings. He knew the hotel business would have been more lucrative than the lounge, so he would have preferred that. He was even present on one of the club's biggest nights. He just wanted to see the women's costumes and bodies, but would put up a front.

"Sage, looks like it's gonna be a great night for business tonight. The line is around the building! What's going on tonight? I might have to stick around and help out," Mr. Kline commented.

As I grabbed another bottle of liquor, I replied, "Yes, tonight's going to be bananas! It is still early and the place is jumping. We are having a Halloween party tonight that's why everyone has on costumes."

He remarked, "Is it that time of year again? Man, time flies by so quickly. These years are really zooming by. Sage, you have to enjoy them while you can."

"That's right sir," I said.

He walked away in the direction of the dance floor peering at every female in the building. He came to the lounge every night on the big event nights and acted like he didn't know what was going on. He loved the women and always fronted like he didn't. I personally never liked the way he talked down to Mrs. Kline. She was such a sweet lady and deserved respect. His only strength over her was his litigious nature. They owned the lounge equally together when they were married, but during the divorce the ownership percentages were divided into three parts. Mrs. Kline, Mr. Kline, and their daughter Jasmine were all owners of the lounge. The judge gave Jasmine a piece of Mr. Kline's ownership. He was very upset by that because he could no longer impose his will on the lounge's decisions even if he wanted to.

I ran the small bar that night because it was closest to the dance floor. It was my favorite bar to work because I loved to see the patrons dancing and having a good time. Additionally, if I needed to leave for a minute to grab something or resolve an issue, I was free to do so because this was the small bar. "Party Ain't a Party" was blasting through all speakers near the dance floor. That song had the crowd pumping and everyone was having a good time, even Mr. Kline and his hypocritical self. The crowd was infused with electricity like it had been hit by Thor's electric bolt when they heard the DJ about to drop "Fiesta" remix. There were bottles in the air and guys were spitting their best game at the women so they can leave with them and have a happy ending.

"I have been looking for you all night and I have finally found you," one guy said to a woman.

"Now that you have found me, you should buy me a drink. I want to get tipsy," she replied.

He screamed, "Bartender. Get her one of whatever she wants! It's on me."

She replied, "That's very sweet of you. I appreciate it. Thanks."

"Here it is. I'm sweet to you, but you never text me. That's a shame how you return my generosity," he remarked.

She looked at her friend and they both start laughing. They both started laughing because his remark was quite comical. It was humorous because they had never met until then. He used that line about texting to "Transfer" into a conversation about her phone number. This was a lot easier and less forward than coming straight out and asking for her number. He was more likely to be rejected with no clever plan.

She replied, "You never texted me either, so you are just as guilty as me."

Before you knew it, he was putting her number in his phone and buying her another drink. All of the guys in the spot were scoping the lounge. Their eyes were moving from one side to the other as they looked for prey. They also transferred physically around the club. This is also referred to as "The Transfer" and is not something that is haphazardly done. The constant transferring of these guys was for very specific reasons. One reason they look around is to find a spot where the most available women are. They want to be where they have the best chance of picking up someone. Some dudes will choose the bar while others will choose the dance floor. Dudes physically move around the club because they will bump into more women that way. Also, moving around keeps them from getting caught. For example, if a dude got a woman's number while she was at the bar, he will go to another area of the venue and get another woman's number. The lady sitting at the bar will most likely never know what he was up to. Dude will be able to scoop up more numbers by being on the go. "The Transfer" is also why men tend to club hop. If one spot is not jumping, they will go to another spot in hopes of finding women. It is really very similar to how animals hunt. They will scope and scrutinize until they find what they want. It's unfortunate, but women are simply prey to a lot of men.

The costumes of the customers got more risqué, bizarre, and ridiculous as the clock ticked. One guy was supposed to be Michael Jackson. He was wearing a replica of the jacket Michael Jackson wore in Thriller, a fake diamond glove, and high-water pants. The only problem with his costume was that he had his entire body painted white to really look like Michael Jackson. To make matters worse, he had started to sweat and it looked like he was sweating milk. One girl who was wearing a trench coat and flip flops had everyone's attention. She had my attention because it was freezing outside, but she had on flip flops. Even the females were wondering what her costume was. I guessed that she was Bonnie from "Bonnie and Clyde". The trench coat she was wearing was similar to the one Bonnie was wearing in the old "Bonnie and Clyde" movie.

"Let me guess…You are Bonnie, right? So where is Clyde? Is he out robbing a bank or something? I hope you're not going to rob us tonight," I remarked jokingly.

She stated, "Not even close, but I guess the coat would make you say that."

In a confused tone I asked, "What is your costume then?"

"I have the best costume in the building. It is simple and over the top at the same time. The simplicity of it is brilliance," she announced to me and some other spectators.

What she did next was shocking to me and everyone else standing around. The lady kicked off her flip flops into the crowd of people. One flip flop hit a female customer clear in the forehead.

"You wanna see my costume?" asked the lady. "Who wants to see it?"

The whole crowd started screaming and she gave them what they asked for. The lady planted her feet and took the belt off her coat. She began to unbutton her coat and snatched it off expeditiously.

"I am a new born baby! This is my birthday suit! Do you like it? Do you love it?" she questioned loudly.

I had never seen anything like that before.

The male customers screamed for her to twerk. Some of female patrons begged for her to put her coat back on. I hollered for security. The security guards rushed over and threw her coat back on her naked body and immediately removed her from the premises.

"That is the most outrageous costume or non-costume I have ever seen," I said to Mrs. Kline.

Mrs. Kline said, "I almost threw up right on the spot when she disrobed. Some people are so uncouth. I would never do anything like that. That poor young girl should have more respect for herself. Can't believe she thought that was a good idea. Just put all her goods on display."

Even Mrs. Kline's daughter, Jasmine thought the birthday suit was way over the top. She was in her early twenties and had a pretty open mind when it came to many things. She was at the lounge regularly with her friends, although she didn't enjoy the scene. They normally came in and just had a few drinks. Jasmine's entire clique was drop dead gorgeous. They always garnered plenty attention and that night was the same as always. They were turning down guys down left and right.

I remember years ago when me and Jasmine first got really cool. She told me how she was tired of meeting guys at the lounge and was looking for a stable dude who wasn't into the club and bar scene.

Jasmine said, "I have been around the clubs

and bars so for long that they have become pedestrian to me. I really want a change of pace. Dudes into the club scene are all the same. Kinda wanna get away and experience a new culture and hopefully meet some more refined guys, but I know my mom needs me here. That's the only reason I still come around as often as I do."

I explained, "Sometimes you have to live for yourself. You can't spend your entire life living for someone else. If you do that, you aren't really living. You're essentially acting a part that someone has scripted for you."

"That's exactly how I feel. I need to find myself. I feel like my folks have too much say so and influence over my life," she stated. "I'm like a puppet. I really want to get out and see the world."

I articulated, "You need to get empowered. You will not be happy unless you do. You do not want to end up as a bitter old lady who let life pass her by. Get on it!"

It was one in the morning and I had a client to meet. She came to the lounge and met me in my office. I knew it was a conflict of interest to have an appointment with people at the lounge, but I really didn't have any other choice. I was always at the lounge, so it was just ideal that we met there. I wondered if Mrs. Kline would have a problem with what I was doing. I didn't ask because she may have told me to shut it down. It wasn't like I was doing anything illegal. Besides, I normally offered advice anyway and was finally getting paid to do it. Ever since I helped the daughter of a local politician named Sadie, things had been rolling. She turned to social media and shouted me out. She really advertised how I helped her. She even attributed her blossoming marriage to the advice I gave her. Because of that, all of her friends and family came to the lounge for tips about various things and they brought deep pockets with them. They paid me well and spent a lot of money at the lounge. It was almost like I was a practicing Relationship Counselor. Not only that, people who heard about me from social media stopped by all the time. Normally they wanted relationship advice and I gave plenty of it.

It was by sheer luck that I met Sadie because we actually met at the lounge on my day off. One day, a while ago, I stopped by the lounge to grab my books for class. Luckily, at the same time that I was walking in, so was this pleasant smelling young lady. I complimented her on how great she smelled.

I said, "I love your perfume. What fragrance is that?"

Sadie stated, "Thank you very much. It's called Gautier for women. I like this fragrance and men seem to like it too."

I remarked, "I'm sure you can't keep them off of you! Your calendar is probably booked solid."

"No, unfortunately it is not. It's pretty empty

right now. That's why I am in here solo. I don't have any trouble meeting men, but I do have trouble keeping them," Sadie said.

"What's that about?" I asked.

"I don't know. Every time I meet a guy, he seems to be the perfect man and then he turns out to be a blank. It's like I've met my prince charming. He does all the things I could ever imagine and then nothing," she narrated angrily.

I replied, "Tell me about your initial meetings with these guys. What's the conversation about? Is he dominating the conversation, or are you?"

"Well, I normally do most of the talking. I am very independent and outgoing. I like to let the guys know exactly where I am coming from. I really don't have time to play games, so I am straight forward with them," she eagerly replied.

"That may be exactly what your problem is," I told her.

Sadie worded, "Umm, excuse me! I am not the problem! They just can't handle a woman who is driven, self-sufficient, and knows what she wants."

I quickly replied, "No, no sister. Not saying that you are the problem, but your approach may be."

"Well, what do you mean?" Sadie interrogated promptly.

I answered, "What you are doing is called the 'Declaration'. A declaration is an emphatic statement or an announcement of some sort.

The "Declaration" is when you make an announcement to the guy you are talking to. The announcement is like a 'here I am' statement or 'this is me' statement. During this time, you are letting the guy know what you are about and what you are looking for."

In theory, The "Declaration" is a great idea. It may seem like it's a good idea to openly communicate your intentions and expectations to a guy upfront. I get it. You have been trained to do so by many people over the years. Unfortunately, that is a misconception. You could actually leave yourself open and subject to hurt feelings.

I compare the "Declaration" to playing a game of Spades. In the game of Spades, there four individuals paired together into two teams. Each player has thirteen cards to help them make books. The highest card takes the book and the books basically equal points. One important part of the game is to keep people from knowing the cards in your hand. If the opposite team knows your cards, they will have the upper hand because they will know what card to play. Knowing what to play will allow them to make books and move them closer to winning the game.

Another scenario to keep in mind is this. Imagine two countries going to war against one another. Before the war starts, one country decides to tell the other country what its strategy will be to win the war. The opposing country will obviously take that information and use it to win the war. Now let us compare this to dating and meeting people. I have seen many instances of the "Declaration" going the wrong way for women. That is why I advise women to initially stay away from it. When you meet a man for the first time, he has nothing to go off of, but your physical attributes. He may be attracted to your hair, buttocks, but ultimately, he doesn't know you to like anything else about you. Men lust first and love second.

When men and women meet for the first time it can be an exciting time, but it can also be a little bit nerve-wracking. It is often exciting because it is new and fresh. Contrarily, it can be awkward because you don't know quite what to say and don't want to offend the other person. The beginning of a relationship is also a time when people are learning about one another. Women have the upper hand during this time. They really are in the driver's seat because the man is pursuing her.

The "Declaration" removes the edge that women have. The man would normally have to figure out what the woman wants. During the time a man is figuring out what the female wants, the female can observe the man to see if he's worthy. Since he doesn't know what you want, all of his actions will be genuine. On the other hand, if you tell him everything you want, all he has to do is play the part for a while. Eventually, he will have you thinking that he is the perfect gentlemen when really, he's plotting. In this situation, the woman would have equipped him with a cheat sheet to her test. She doesn't have to be dishonest with him, but just don't tell him everything she's looking for because he could easily follow the script. Of course, she'll have to communicate with him on that level at some point, but just not day one. No man should be entrusted with crucial information like that before she knows he can be trusted. Remember men lust first and love second. He will use her words to get into her bed.

"Sage, that's way too much for me. A piece of kitty cat can't be that serious. Y'all be doing too much. I can't...I can't," Sheena says.

I remark, "Yeah, to you it's too much, but to a lot of fellas, the effort is well worth the effort, time, and energy."

I never did make it to class that day. I got so caught up in our conversation that class was not even a thought. It was worth it though. I was glad to offer some assistance to her. It was both intrinsically and extrinsically rewarding. Through helping one person with a troubling time, I made some very influential connections. I met bankers, senators, real estate moguls, and judges and they all knew me on a first name basis.

"So, what happened at the meeting?" Sheena asks.

"Let me tell you," I respond.

To my surprise, my meeting was very short. I didn't mind that at all. I was used to relationship counseling meetings being long and drawn out. Fortunately for me, the meeting I had to attend was with people who were direct and to the point. It only lasted about thirty minutes. That was great because the lounge was having its busiest Halloween Party ever. It was also great because those thirty minutes made my future even clearer. I remember how I hustled back to the bar by the DJ booth, so I could relieve some of long lines at the other bars. The music was still going strong and the crowd was still dancing and drinking the night away. What was even better about that party was there hadn't been any altercations besides the lady in her birthday suit. We were doing our best to escape the night without any drama. Our security force was pretty fortified and everyone was well schooled on what to do if any ominous situations were to arise.

As the night went on, I wondered what time we would get out of there. I was having fun, but time wasn't going by very quickly. It was probably because it was still technically work for me and I knew the night wasn't over until the lounge was empty. I still had to help clean the place up and prep for the next day's early crowd. In addition to cleaning up, it was customary for the team to have a meeting after the club closed. We would discuss what went wrong and how to prevent it from happening again. Naturally, we'd discuss what went right and how to build on its success. To cap off the night, we'd divide up the tips. We saved dividing the tips for last because many people would come up with excuses to leave after they got their share and not finish helping with the work. Fortunately, the night ended with no major occurrences. We even got out of the after-work staff meeting early because Mrs. Kline let everybody write down their discussion items to be addressed later. All we had to do was count tips that night. The staff loved Mrs. Kline as much as I did because she was always making kind gestures to the staff.

"Sage, tonight would not have been the success it was without your vision. You had every detail of the night planned out. Your meticulous nature and ability to keep everybody on point were key to the great night. It seems like most people came tonight to see you," Mrs. Kline announced.

I delivered sincerely, "Thanks, but it was a complete team effort. We can't have success if we are not all on the same wavelength. Your direction and allowing us to be here is what made this possible."

She just smiled and walked out the door for the night. It didn't make sense for me to leave since I had to be there early for our weekly delivery trucks, so I made my way to my room in the back of the club. That's how it is when you are a salaried employee. I didn't mind one bit.

That was just more knowledge for me.

My phone began ringing and broke the silence of the night and woke me up as I was dosing off. Mrs. Kline's name was flashing across the screen. I quickly answered the phone because I just knew something was wrong.

"Hello Mrs. Kline. Is everything ok?" I anxiously asked.

She said, "Yes, all is well. Why do you ask?"

"I didn't expect you to call this late, especially after you just left a short time ago," I replied.

She stated, "I know. Sorry, I startled you. I want to meet with you sometime tomorrow and discuss some things that are on my mind for the future of the lounge. It's rather important, so I figured I would contact you immediately before you made plans."

"I will be free after the deliveries for tomorrow come in. We can talk then," I told her.

"Sounds good. I will be free all day, so just call me when everything's complete. I'll come by then," she informed me.

I fell back asleep immediately. In what seemed like an hour, I awoke to the delivery man pounding on the door. The deliveries arrived right on time. I processed the paperwork and sent the delivery man on his way. I tied up some other loose ends and gave Mrs. Kline a call. Not too long later, I heard Mrs. Kline's heels clicking on the floor and her keys jingling against one another. Her face was all business, which was different for her. Mrs. Kline normally had her warm and inviting face on, but I wasn't worried. We sat inside the lounge at our usual meeting booth.

I asked, "What's on your mind that you wanted to meet? Is Mr. Kline pestering you about the lounge again?"

She replied, "Yes, he is always bothering me about the lounge. He still wants to dump the place, but that's never going to change. However, that's not why I wanted to meet with you today. I wanted to discuss my potential future plans for the lounge. You know this place is doing very well now."

"Yes, I do," I replied.

She explained, "Many people have been asking about buying the place, but I don't want to sell it. My plans are definitely not to sell it, but I am considering opening up more locations. I think there is a lot of money to be made by expanding. I'm seriously looking into opening up another location in Miami. I feel there is room for growth for In the Mix. I am trying to think out of the box and keep the lounge moving forward. Unfortunately, I do have concerns about making such a large-scale move. I will make a decision for sure though."

"I think that is a great idea. Growth is what it is all about. If the opportunity presents itself, I think you should move forward with it. Sounds like a fantastic endeavor," I said.

"Sage, I want you to be a part of every move we make. Your leadership and vision are and will be valuable assets to the lounge's current and future success. You are partly the reason why we have had the financial success we have experienced. I don't want to forge forward without you," she remarked.

"I plan to be a part of all the future happenings and successes of the lounge. I am honored to be considered a part of such an esteemed organization. I will do my best to ensure things flow as smoothly as they have been, if not better," I voiced.

"Very good. Do you have any questions for me?" she asked.

"Yes, I do. I don't know if it would be considered a favor or a question, but I will ask anyway. Is there any way I can have some ownership in the lounge? Not much, just a small percent, so that way I can really benefit financially from the moves that are going to take place. I don't want to work my whole life if I don't have to," I spoke.

She answered, "I understand where you are coming from. You have dedicated a lot of your time to keeping the lounge growing and being a place where people want to spend their money. For that, I think you should be rewarded. I have no problem with you owning a small percentage."

Mrs. Kline told me that we would sit down with her lawyer and my lawyer to make sure we both understand what the paper work states. My lawyer is a friend who I met while working the bar one night. The night I met him, he was at the lounge ordering drink after drink. Once he had what I considered to be too many drinks, I stopped serving him. He actually cursed me out for not continuing to serve him. Additionally, I lifted his car keys off the bar when he was trying to pay his tab. He didn't leave until it was time for me to go home. He ended up catching a ride with me. On the way to his house, we ran into a police sobriety check point. James thanked me over and over for driving him home. He knew that would have been stress he didn't need and could have ended his career. Ever since that night, James vowed to be my attorney if I ever needed one.

It was a month after the conversation with Mrs. Kline when I attained three percent ownership of the lounge. Mrs. Kline could only afford to give me three percent of her ownership percentage stake and I was elated that she gave me the maximum that she could. That move put me one step closer to achieving my goal. My plans were finally coming to fruition. All of my hard work was paying off. The excitement I felt was like no other. The only time I had been that happy was high school graduation. I remembered the conversation my mom and I had that day.

"Son, I know you are excited about graduating today. I want you to know that this day is upon you now because of your hard work and willingness to stay the course. Remember in all your future endeavors to put God first and He will make all of your dreams come true," Mom said.

That was my mom. She always had words of encouragement for everything. Every wise word also had a relation to God. It didn't matter if we were having good times or bad times, Ma's message was always unwavering.

She would say, "There are no shortcuts to accomplishing your dreams. What you put into something you will get out."

I always listened to what my mom said because things worked out the way she said they would. In a lot of ways, Mrs. Kline and my mom were very similar. There was not a dishonest bone in either one of their bodies. Also, both of them would offer you whatever assistance they could. All sorts of thoughts floated through my head as the time to sign drew closer. My hands and nose were sweating profusely.

I heard a car pull up in front of the lounge about fifteen minutes to one. I knew it was James because he told me that he would arrive early so we could run through the process of the meeting. James was always on point. When he said something was going to happen, it happened. James told me the process would not be very long because he had already previewed the paperwork and it all looked good. About fifteen minutes after James arrived, I heard more cars pull up and car doors opening and closing. Seconds later, I heard Mrs. Kline's keychain jangling like they always did as she walked through the front door with her attorney.

James said, "Good afternoon. How is everyone doing on this lovely day?"

Mrs. Kline replied warmly, "It's a blessed day. I am excited about the present and future."

"I am too," I enthusiastically stated.

Walter, who was Mrs. Kline's lawyer, was all business and he immediately suggested that we get the paperwork signed and wrapped up. That was not a problem with me because I wanted to hurry the process too. I didn't have anywhere to go, but in my opinion the only way for this to be real to me is, for the paperwork to be signed. Mrs. Kline had never been one to go back on her word, but you can't count your chickens before they hatch. That's the way my mom raised us.

"Nothing is official until you have it in writing. When you pay a bill make sure you get a receipt because people will try to get over on you if you let them," Ma said a million times too many.

Ma raised us to be meticulous in all things that we do. I still hear her classic line that referred to anything we ever did, wanted to do, or planned to do.

"If you gonna do it, do it right. Otherwise, don't do it," she would say.

I hadn't heard those words in quite some time,

but they make me laugh whenever I think of them.

The meeting was completely professional. There was no small talk. Everything we discussed was related to my minority ownership and what my role will be once things were settled with going public and expanding. There was a lot of lawyer talk that I didn't understand, but everything was going just as James said it would. Within an hour, we all signed the paperwork in the appropriate places. I had just become a minority owner of In the Mix. My demeanor was all business, but inside, I really wanted to scream with joy. I was like a hog in slop. I knew proper decorum was to be displayed for such a solemn event, so I held my emotions in check. That day meant so much to me that I even went and bought a brand new suit for it. My mom was at the meeting as well to serve as a witness, but I really just wanted her there to take part in my special moment. After the signing concluded, I had some other non-contractual things I wanted to talk to Mrs. Kline about.

"Mrs. Kline, I thank you again for the opportunity. I have one more request before the meeting is complete," I said.

She replied, "You are welcome and what is it you request?"

"I'm hoping that we can keep me being a minority owner between us. I don't want the staff to know because it may affect my relationship with them," I vocalized.

She commented, "Sure, that's not a problem with me. How do you think it will affect things?"

"Well, I have a fantastic rapport with everyone on staff and I hope to keep it that way. I don't want them to find out about my new status and treat me differently. They may be intimidated or feel they cannot come to me as they have in the past," I explained.

"Sage, I understand your point. This is our business, so nobody needs to know anyway. You won't hear a peep out of me about it. I can assure you that if anybody knows, it will be because you told him or her, not because of me," Mrs. Kline assured.

"Thanks for understanding," I replied as we exited the meeting.

I knew I had taken a huge step forward by finally being able to own something that was lucrative. I remember going to the Sports Park on Route 22 in Jersey as a teenager. It seemed like yesterday when me and my boys had conversations of owning something. It didn't matter if it was the Sports Park, a movie theater, or a bowling alley, we just wanted to own something. Back then, it really seemed like a fantasy. We just talked about things like that, but never really thought it could happen to people like us. We wanted to be able to throw money like the rappers did in videos or drive nice cars like the Hollywood stars. We hoped we could make it big at something and have expendable cash to take trips with and hopefully help people out of bad situations. Despite what many may have thought, we didn't want money to flash around town. Unfortunately, not everybody thinks like that. Some people like to do harm when they have surplus funds.

One night, the lounge hosted a Fourth of July party and the it was packed. There wasn't any standing room on the dance floor because the place was mobbed. The only places to stand were either behind the bar, in the reserved seating areas, and the (VIP) area. I remember thinking why anyone would spend all of that money just to sit in a place for a few hours. It didn't make any sense to me. There were also guys in the lounge that night buying rounds of drinks. Needless to say, I didn't want them to stop because that was how I got paid, but it was still strange to me. These guys were also in the lounge making it rain. It seemed like certain songs really promoted the throwing of money. When the "Get Money" track came on, it was like the lounge was filled with millionaires, but it surely was not. Every dude in the club could seemingly relate to the song. It all came together in the blink of an eye.

Earlier in the evening, before the lounge was crowded, this tall, thin, dark-skinned dude arrived.

"It's still kinda early. We won't get packed for at least another hour," I said.

He replied, "The earlier, the better because it is cheaper to get in when you come early. Plus, I am not one for long lines. This way I don't have to wait in line to get in and I don't have to wait all day to order a drink."

"Makes sense to me," I told him. "You win all the way around."

I really thought that made sense because I would employ the same strategy when I went to places. I liked to be inside the place when it gets packed as opposed to being on line when the party is blasting off. I remember the guy paying for his eight dollar drink with seven raggedy one dollar bills and some coins to make up for the difference. I knew for sure he was broke because he didn't leave a tip either. Later on, the same dude was back at the bar about to buy another drink. By that time, the bar was filled with women on each side of him. I was expecting another limp set of bills and some change, but that wasn't close to what happened. This time around, he pulled out a wad of cash to pay for his drink. This guy had all of his large bills on top. He flipped through the entire mountain of cash just to pull out a ten dollar bill. Surprisingly, he even let me keep the change as a tip. It was almost like this was a totally different dude.

When I saw the faces of the women who were sitting at the bar, I knew what was going on. This was part of the game called "The Intrigue". It all came full circle as to why these dudes were in here spending money at such an excessive rate. It was all for the "Intrigue". The word intrigue means to arouse interest or curiosity and to fascinate. During the "Intrigue", a man will do whatever he can to draw you in. He may wear his best clothes and make sure he is immaculately groomed. Additionally, he may even have the real expensive car with all the bells and whistles. Men have many preconceived notions about women. One thought men have is that women will flock to money. That is why the guy at the lounge pulled out that wad of cash. He was banking on intriguing the women with his money. If the Intrigue" is done properly, a woman will approach the guy or it will be a lot easier for the man to approach her. The abundance of cash he possesses makes him appealing because it makes him seem stable. He's also hoping to touch a superficial side of a woman if she has one. His plan is for her to think about what she can get out of the guy.

Another definition of intrigue is a secret plan that is detrimental to someone. The "Intrigue" is definitely detrimental. It can be harmful to the woman because the man will use his cash to woo and mislead her, but once he gets what he wants, it's over. The wining and dining will stop out of the blue. He will no longer care about being dressed up around her. He will be like a totally different person. His overall goal is sex. If the man has serious intentions for the female, then the last thing he would want to gamble on is if her intentions are genuine. He would rather the female like him for who he is as a person. After he has established that she's genuine, then he won't mind spoiling her with his finances. Women should be careful of any man who exposes large amounts of cash and promises gifts when she doesn't even know him. It's all part of "The Intrigue".

"Since you have all that extra, you should buy me a drink too," said one of the women sitting at the bar.

The guy asked, "What do you and your girls want to drink?"

Before they could answer, I heard the man calling me over.

In a calm voice he stated, "Get them whatever they want. It's on me."

His stunt seemed to work because the women were locked into him. Before the night was over, he was on the dance floor with one of them. They didn't separate for the rest of the night and even left together. He may have gotten the happy ending he was looking for.

CHAPTER 3

I had been a minority owner for months before I told my brother. When I finally told him about my fortuitous happening with the lounge, he started screaming at the top of his lungs through the phone.

"You know you are in the owner's box now. Don't get brand new on us small guys and pretend you do not know us anymore. You did it, bro. I'm proud of you," he said.

That was always his style. He celebrated everything good that I did. He had always been a real supportive dude. It was as if he was living my successes with me. Sometimes it seemed like he was more excited than I was about good things that happened to me. I remember how he acted after I graduated from high school. He did cart wheels and back flips when they called my name during the ceremony. He also said something else to me that was totally expected when I told him the news about my promotion.

"You know that new deal you struck with the club is going to mean a lot more money for your bank account. You know what comes along with more money?" he asked.

I said, "Yes, I know the song. More problems."

He replied, "No, man. Money will help get rid of your problems. More women is what you will have."

That was Dave. He was always thinking of ways to meet women or have his next conquest. I knew the pleasures a woman can physically and emotionally afford me, but I never thought it was worth the amount of effort guys put into it. Men spend countless hours trying to get women in the sack. It seemed to me to be a tremendous amount of work for a few moments in time. I always felt like they should put more effort into having families or working to build a secure future. He would have been at the lounge the night I gained partnership, but he was at the hospital waiting for his first child to arrive. Our conversation got cut short that night because of drama.

I knew I had to go above and beyond with my efforts at the lounge. I became even more meticulous in everything I did. Mrs. Kline and In the Mix were relying on me more than ever. I was eager to get back to work and did not leave until all "Ts" were crossed and "Is" were dotted. I had to let Mrs. Kline know that I was extremely grateful for the opportunity she had provided me. Mrs. Kline walked past my office at the exact moment I realized I needed to bring something to her attention.

"Mrs. Kline, can I have a few minutes of your time?" I asked.

"Sure, you can have a few minutes. Meet me in my office. I'm expecting a phone call and don't want to miss it," she said.

Shortly after I was made partner, I asked Mrs. Kline if I could get a monthly expense report for the lounge. I wanted to see if there were any ways we could increase our profit margins. Even before I was made partner, I would try to find ways to save the lounge money. Of course, at the point that I was a partner, I was extremely concerned with expenses. This affected my bottom line at the end of the month. Three percent of whatever the club profits each month could be a lot or a little depending on how much the lounge brought in.

"I have some numbers I want to crunch with you," I said as I sat in Mrs. Kline's office.

She replied, "I hope the numbers you want to crunch add up to more profits for us."

We both laughed out loud. Even though we laughed at her joke, the truth is that she was very serious. She wasn't all about profits, but she liked them. Let's be honest, she was in business to make money.

"But seriously, what do you have?" she asked.

"I have scrutinized the lounge's monthly expenses over the last few months and want to share with you my findings," I voiced.

"I see," she said.

"I believe we can save in several different areas. We can reduce spending by ten percent on supplies. We can also save seven percent on staff related costs. Lastly, we can bank money on utility bills. I am putting a plan together to make these things possible and will present it to you upon its completion," I explained.

"Sounds great! I will wait for your presentation, but I do want to be certain of one thing. I don't want any changes to compromise the integrity of our service, staff, or any aspect of the lounge," she uttered firmly.

"Oh, no worries Mrs. Kline. I would never jeopardize your establishment," I worded. "I feel everything will be the same, except for the overhead expenditures."

Thursday nights at the lounge were always a good time. They were pleasant nights to work because the crowd was always steady, but not as boisterous as Friday, Saturday, and Sunday nights. The best part about it was that the money I made was not usually much different. We basically made the same amount of money for far less work and hassle. Thursday nights also allowed for more interaction with the clients. One good thing about Thursday nights was that they were predictable. Nothing out of the ordinary ever happened on Thursdays until this one Thursday when that all changed.

One of the bartenders who normally worked on Thursday nights called out, so we were one bartender short. I had no intentions on working the bar that night, but had no choice because we were short-handed. I had more experience than the other bartenders, so I let them work the big bar as a team, while I worked the small bar by myself. One night when I was tending the bar a girl I used to go to college with came in the lounge by herself. I thought that was strange because I had never seen her alone before.

As she walked in, we made eye contact and she promptly headed in my direction at the bar. I thought to myself that she was going to ask for some free drinks. As she approached me, I thought of three different ways to tell her that she wouldn't be getting anything free from me. My main objective was to be as polite as possible. This is a business and the last thing I wanted was to make her mad. She was in a sorority, was a gorgeous woman, and had tons of friends on campus. I didn't want to rub her the wrong way and cause the business to take a hit because of it. I concluded that I'd make a nice gesture by buying her first drink. I couldn't remember her name at first, but I remembered that it was Liz just as she reached the bar.

I asked, "What up Liz? What are you doing in here without your friends?"

"Hey Sage! Ain't much up. I just came to chill by myself tonight. Sometimes I like to separate from the pack and do my own thing," Liz answered.

"Aye, I feel you on that. I'm by myself all the time unless I'm in here. Well, damn I'm always in here now that I think about it, but it's all good. Gotta work to eat. Ain't nobody giving me nothing," I orated.

She replied, "I'm with my sorors so much that I never have a moment to myself, so I didn't even tell them I was stepping out tonight. I be needing my space."

"I can dig it. Ya first drink is on me. Just let me know what you want and when you want it," I offered.

"That's sweet of you! Well, since you offered, let me get some tequila. I don't want anything mixed with it. No ice or anything… I want it straight," Liz voiced.

I fixed Liz's drink and we conversed for quite some time. Liz and I conversed about everything from politics to campus issues to our home towns. While we chatted, she ordered another shot of tequila and I could tell the two drinks were impacting her. Liz seemed to have a very nice buzz. She wasn't drunk and I couldn't allow her to get that way, so I didn't serve her any more alcohol. One of Liz's favorite songs came on and she began dancing to it seductively. She was looking at me the entire time she danced. Three songs later she made it back over to the bar.

"I'm thirsty as hell Sage!" Liz stated. "Give me a drink!"

"I'll give you a drink, but it's going to be water, cranberry juice, or a soda, but it's not going to be alcoholic," I stated firmly.

Liz replied, "I don't want any of those. I want something sweet. I know you have something sweet back there."

"Oh yeah, I have something for you. Give me a second and I'll hook up something sweet and non-alcoholic for you," I told.

I mixed up a fruit punch drink for Liz. It was slightly slushy too. I prepared it that way to hopefully give her something sweet and that would cool her off a bit. She was sweating a good bit from the two drinks and from dancing. Liz leaned up against the bar as she drank my equivalent of a fruit punch Slurpee from Seven Eleven. She started slurping it from the straw, but stopped. She removed the straw and began guzzling it straight from the cup. She swallowed the drink it three big gulps. Liz was clearly thirsty.

"Damn, you want another one?" I asked.

"Thanks, but I'm good. Honestly, it wasn't sweet enough for me. I know you got something sweeter than that," Liz shot back.

"Yeah, I can make you a cold sweet ass glass

of sugar water if you want. Just say the word and I'll get you right," I commented jokingly.

"I don't want no damn sugar water. I ain't no damn Bebe kid, but I know you got something sweet I can drink," Liz retorted.

I pretty much knew that she was talking slick, but I couldn't tell if she was serious or joking. Even if she was serious, I couldn't act on it now. There it was, I was minding my business and she was coming on to me. I played dumb like I didn't know what she was talking about. My best bet was to not engage her and maybe she'd chill out. Boy was I wrong! It seemed like she thought I was playing hard to get and it made her try harder. She leaned forward on the bar and whispered to me.

"I want to taste your dick," Liz uttered while she seductively caressed her finger with her tongue.

Liz was an easy ten out of ten on the beauty scale and her body was right there to match. My dick even jumped a little bit when she said she wanted to give me head. I was never one to mix business with pleasure. In my opinion, the two just don't belong together. I laughed it off, but Liz wasn't laughing or smirking. She was as serious as a heart attack. What she did next really surprised me. Liz walked over to the side of the bar where the patrons could not see her. Before long, Liz ducked down and crawled into the bar space with me.

I wanted to tell her to get up, but I also didn't want to make a scene, so I allowed her to stay down there. Honestly, part of me wanted her to make good on what she said she wanted to do. I told myself that I wouldn't prompt her to suck my dick, but if she did, I wouldn't stop her. A moment later, I felt Liz tugging at my belt buckle. The thought of me getting my dick sucked from behind the bar with customers there, was both exciting and frightening. It was exciting because the thought of getting caught was prevalent in my mind and added oomph to it. I was scared because I knew if I got caught, I'd have a problem on my hands.

My belt became unbuckled and my pants and underwear were pulled down below my ass cheeks. Liz methodically massaged my balls with her hands. My dick got harder than tungsten. I felt Liz's mouth cover the head of my dick. Liz sucked the head of my dick and then popped it out of her mouth. She repeated that action over and over. I tried not to, but I kept looking down at her because it felt so good. As I looked down at her, she was looking up at me. Her eyes were asking me if I liked what she was doing and my facial expressions were answering that what she was doing was splendid.

Liz began putting more and more of my dick in her mouth each time she went down on it. I felt all of her tongue and lips, but not one bit of her teeth. I noticed that she was sucking my cock to the beat of the song the DJ was playing. At first, I tried not to move much, but I became so engulfed in her head job that I started wiggling my hips and slowly fucked her mouth.

To my horror, Mrs. Kline noticed me looking down and started walking toward me. I knew she'd come behind the bar if she walked over here, so I had to stop Liz. I wouldn't be able to explain why I was getting my dick sucked during work hours at the bar. I had to think quickly. I called out for Mrs. Kline to start dancing. Fortunately, she paused in embarrassment for a moment. I told the DJ to switch the song to the Electric Slide to appease Mrs. Kline and he did so. Many people who weren't dancing got up to dance. While everyone was twisting and turning to the song, I grabbed Liz by the back of the head and fucked her face. It looked as if I was dancing to the song, but in reality, I was chasing a nut. Liz's head was hitting the shelving unit of the bar, but she didn't flinch. I nutted in her mouth and she swallowed every bit of it.

"Now, that drink was sweet enough for me Sage. That's exactly what I was looking for to quench my thirst," Liz said.

I smiled as I looked down at her. I pulled my draws and pants up. She waited for the people dancing to have their backs to the bar before she resurfaced. Liz stood back at the bar as if she hadn't just sucked my dick and swallowed my nut. I thanked her for doing that and she walked off.

Mrs. Kline had enough dancing and walked over to the bar to tell me that she was leaving.

"I wasn't going to walk over to you, but you were looking down and I couldn't get your attention when I was waving," Mrs. Kline spoke.

"Yeah, I was looking down, but it turned out to be *nuttin* serious," I remarked.

Mrs. Kline left for the night. Hell, all I remembered thinking was that I had to misdirect her attention. I had to get Mrs. Kline's attention off of me otherwise I would have been caught. The rest of the night was uneventful and panned out to be just like any other Thursday night at the lounge. I was caught off guard on how willing Liz was to give me head and it made me remember an old class session.

I immediately thought of a PowerPoint presentation I had to give in one of my classes. My topic of discussion was relationships and why men cheat. It led to a fantastic conversation for the class. It seemed like female students were extremely interested in the results of my research. Many people in the class were shocked to find out why 93 percent of the men I surveyed revealed why they cheat. Before giving up the answer, I asked my female classmates what they thought the reason was. Many of them thought the answer was they were unhappy at home or that the man's significant other wasn't providing the sexual pleasures they were seeking. Some of them even thought that maybe it was something the women were lacking in themselves. Those answers did show up as a small percentage of my findings, but overall, they were negligible.

The answer actually rested within the dude. What I mean is that the reason why most of them said they cheated had nothing to do with anyone else, but them. Their views of cheating were what lead them to cheat. The men didn't view sex as being something that was very important. Men consider sex to be something recreational. Many cited having sex as being something to do to pass time, but it wasn't for keeps and wasn't cherished by them. Even many of the guys in the class, stated that hooking up with women was similar to shooting a game of pool on a Saturday night. It merely serves as a fun time and holds no weight. This makes it easier for them to cheat because there's no emotional connection needed for them to commit the act. Essentially, a man with views like this, only needs the opportunity to cheat.

The class was in an uproar after I reported my findings. Everyone in the class had an opinion about what I found. Hands were raised to ask questions and side bar conversations were dominating the class. Things eventually got back to order once the professor reigned everyone in. This topic had clearly struck a nerve. I always loved that class because we had the most interesting discussions and research topics. I actually was put in the hot seat when the professor asked me a question about my presentation.

He asked, "Sage, what is your opinion of your research findings? Did you find your research cases to be genuine?"

I responded, "I really didn't think they were genuine in their responses. My overall opinion is that men use that as an excuse to justify their infidelities. It is really just a cover story for men not to own up to bigger issues they have. One being an inability to control themselves and having a total disregard for the person they're dating. They clearly want their cake and ice cream too. Their responses were not genuine because when I asked them, if they thought their mates cheating was a big deal, they all responded "Yes". That proved to me that sex to them is more than something to do to just pass the time. I also found that most men are hypocrites."

CHAPTER 4

Early one morning, Jasmine showed up at the lounge totally unexpectedly and caught me off guard. Her arrival was well before the day's opening time. If it was before opening time, she was never one to pop up at the lounge without calling. She was always respectful and considerate of what other people may be busy doing. When I saw her face peering through the glass door of the lounge, I figured something must have been awry. I quickly rushed to the door and as I opened it, I noticed a very sullen look on her face. I was almost afraid to ask what her problem was, but I knew she needed help. Before I had a chance to ask her what she needed, she spoke to me.

"Sage, I am so glad I caught you. I almost didn't stop by, but I figured you had to be here this close to opening," she said.

I asked, "Why didn't you call me?" Don't you know the best way to get me is to hit my cell?"

She retorted, "Man, I must have called you a hundred times in the last hour."

"Nah, you didn't hit me. My phone is right here on my hip. It did not ring, beep or anything of the sort," I said.

I reached for my phone only to realize that it actually wasn't on me. I checked all of my pockets, but it wasn't there. I really did think I had my phone in my pocket, but obviously I was wrong. I couldn't remember where it was in that moment. I just hoped it wasn't lost for good because I had many contacts in that phone that I couldn't afford to lose.

"I guess I don't have it on me, after all. Maybe that's why I didn't hear it ringing. Oh yeah, I forgot I put it on the charger when the battery got low. My bad," I said.

"Boy, you are terrible. And you were blaming me," Jasmine said, as she laughed at me.

"But what's wrong with you?" I asked.

Jasmine looked surprised and questioned, "How do you know something's wrong with me?"

I promptly replied, "Well let's see. Besides the fact that you admittedly called me a hundred times, showed up here earlier than you ever have in history, your facial expression is a mix between constipation and worry, and your tone gave it away."

"True, I gave it all away that easily. Well, you could always tell when I needed something. I have problems, but I don't know what to do to solve them. I need some advice and I know you are the man for the job," she said.

I asked, "What's going on?"

"Alright, you asked for it. I was approached by Virginia Miller. She's the lady who owns '*Euro World Magazine*'. If you don't know, that is the preeminent magazine of Europe. She wants me to work for her company," Jasmine said.

"Ok, that's great so far. Go for it! She must have really liked your body of work," I stated.

Jasmine vocalized, "It's not so great yet, but I guess it could be. Also, I never submitted my portfolio to her. She heard about my work and sought me out."

I voiced, "Your work must have been impressive! You are double talking though. You said it could it be great and not great at the same time. Please enlighten me."

"For starters, the job is overseas and I would have to move immediately. Secondly, the job does not pay for moving expenses nor do they pay for my living expenses once I get there. I would also need money to live off of until I get my first paycheck. I really don't want to make that move and have myself in a precarious predicament, but I know it's a once in a lifetime opportunity," Jasmine explained.

"Yeah, it does seem like a once in a lifetime opportunity. It seems like your only problem is money, so just tell your mom what's good and that's that. You'll be on your way," I told her.

"Really, Sage! Seriously! You know my mom isn't coming off any money that will enable me to leave the country for good. She is too much of a worrywart for that," Jasmine shot back.

I calmly replied, "Oh yeah, you're right. She barely wants you hanging out at night. Out of the country will be a definite no-no. Still no need to worry. I will give you the money."

"There is no way I am letting you or anybody else give me that much money. I don't like to owe anybody anything, so forget about that," she said.

"Jaz, come on. You know I always have you when you need me to. Now is no different," I said.

"I am not a charity case. Plus, I know you need your bread to make the moves you want to make. I won't let my shortcomings get in your way of success. I came to you to help me strategize not for a handout or to be a burden on you," Jasmine continued.

"Ok, the only other option is drastic, but it may be the answer to make it happen for you," I responded.

"I am all ears. Tell me what you got," Jasmine verbalized enthusiastically.

"You are a beautiful woman. You could

consider stripping and selling your ass?" I worded jokingly.

She looked at me with eyes of molten lava. It was the hottest look that I had ever seen in my life. I saw her facial muscles tighten up. It was like a volcano getting ready to erupt. Only her mouth was the volcano and her words were the scorching hot lava. I cut her off before she had a chance to curse me out.

"Chill Jaz, it was a joke. I just wanted to see you smile," I said.

We both laughed hard to the point where our stomachs started to hurt and we started shedding tears. I'm glad she didn't punch me in the face for my joke. If she had punched me, I would've just had to take that. It probably wouldn't have hurt me anyway because Jasmine is a girly girl. Jasmine's all brains and beauty with no brawn. After the laughter ceased, I told her what I really had in mind.

I asked, "Would you be willing to sell your percent of the lounge in order to make the move?"

"I definitely thought about that. Yes, I would, but I also don't want to give up a stake in the family business," she replied. "Besides, I don't have anyone to sell it to on such short notice. Nobody has cash just lying around and ready to spend."

I vocalized, "The best advice I can offer you is to sell your stake in the lounge. If you sell me your percentage in the lounge, you will have plenty of money to take the job overseas. You will be able to get your apartment, have money to live off of, and get a car to get you back and forth."

She replied, "That still doesn't help me with my concerns over not owning any of the lounge. Not that I don't appreciate your suggestion, but that only gets me half of what I want."

"There is a simple fix to the problem you have. I'll buy your percentage in the lounge and you will take the job overseas and do the things we just discussed. To make it work for you, what I can do is sell you your portion back when you return back to the United States. The lounge will stay in the family. I will be able to make a little extra money while you are gone and you will get to live it up in Europe. Most importantly, you will have peace of mind knowing your interest in the lounge is waiting for you," I explained.

Jasmine was all smiles and thanks after I offered my solution to her problem. She was excited about the new outlook on her future. She would finally be able to leave the pedestrian life of the United States. She was on to bigger and better things and was sincerely appreciative of me for helping her take this huge step in her life. Jasmine was like a sister to me and her happiness meant a lot to me. Her family had been great to me over the years and allowed me to realize many of the things I want out of life.

Jasmine said, "My mom will not be the least bit pleased by this Sage. She is gonna come down on you hard for helping me go so far away from home. You know she barely wants me to go across the street without her. You are really putting yourself in the crossfire."

While shaking my head, I replied, "Yeah, it will be hell to pay, but it is for a good cause. You have to live your life and be happy."

"To help keep you out of the drama, I just won't tell her where I got the money from. That way you won't have to get the ugly looks and cursed out," Jasmine orated.

"I don't want you keeping things from your mom, but that doesn't sound like a bad idea to me," I shot back.

"I understand, but I'm not saying anything. I really don't want to get into all of that with her anyway. She likes to get loud with me when she doesn't get her way. Again, thanks for going out of your way to help me make my dreams come true. I'll let cover you from the drama," Jasmine said.

"Bet, well listen, I'll get my home boy James to draw up the paperwork. He's a corporate attorney, so it'll be a breeze for him to get the documents together. Once he gets the papers drawn up, we'll meet at his office and sign them to make it official. The good thing is he won't even charge us because he's my friend," I worded.

Jasmine thanked me and told me to let her know when she needed to come sign the paperwork. She informed me that we needed to move on the paperwork pretty quickly in order for her to get to Europe for the job. She exited the lounge totally opposite from how she entered. When she arrived, she was a bit sullen and concerned, but she left happy and optimistic. To expedite things, I called James as soon as Jasmine left that day. James said that he'd get everything together for us as soon as he could.

Hours later, two guys came walking into the lounge for some early afternoon recreation. As I was setting up shop for cocktail hour, the two dudes sat at the bar. I greeted them promptly and warmly as I did all patrons of the lounge

I said, "Hello guys, I'm Sage."

"What's up? I'm Sylvester," uttered one guy.

The other man stated, "I'm Lester. Good to meet you."

They wasted no time ordering a couple of drinks and some wings. They apparently didn't want to get caught up in the long wait times once the lounge got packed. They showed a slight degree of common sense for not waiting until the spot was jammed packed to order. I also appreciated them ordering early because it relieved some pressure off of the kitchen staff. The faster we could get the orders in and out, the better.

"You must own the place because you are

always here," remarked Lester.

I replied, "Nah, I am just a highly motivated bartender. Plus, this place is fun. I like being around different people with diverse personalities. This place is pretty free flowing and it allows me to be myself. I don't have to wear suits and be around people who I can't stand like at normal jobs. Plus, this job is very flexible and accommodates my personal life schedule. I just can't beat the fringe benefits."

I really didn't care to tell them any of my personal business because I didn't even know them. Even back then, I wasn't one to tell my personal business to strangers or even friends for that matter. The less people know about me, the better. If they don't know much, they can't hurt me by spreading my business. Sometimes, I would spread false information to different people and see if it comes back to me. That used to make it easy for me to pinpoint who had loose lips and I knew I couldn't trust them.

Sylvester remarked, "Man, you are crazy! There is no way I would spend so many days at work if I didn't own it. Oh, I know what it is. You are getting your compensation through the women. How many are you sleeping with? I know you are seeing plenty of action. I know I would be!"

I didn't cosign any of what the men were saying, but instead I just listened. For me, there really wasn't much to discuss with them. I don't see why men sit around and discuss their sexual prowess. Instead of investing countless man hours in trying to have sex with as many women as possible, I'd rather be investing that time in my future. There really isn't any big accomplishment in having sex with dozens of women. Any misogynist can do that. Now, on the other hand, there is esteem in finding the one you love and building a future with her. I'd much rather focus on that.

"Young man, you should be knocking them down. You're in college and you work here, so I know you're meeting hundreds of women. Treat yourself to fucking a few of them. It's only right considering you're still a young spry man," Lester narrated.

"Thanks for the advice sir, but my goal is to be rich. I find what you're talking about to be a distraction to say the least. Plus, with sex, comes kids and I'm not trying to have any of them anytime," I commented.

Sylvester spoke, "Lester is right youngster. You don't want to get old and feel like you missed out on something, so you should live a little while you're young. Trust me, living with regrets will kick your ass. Remember, you only live once."

"You have access to a variety of women too. All complexions. Chocolate women, redbone women, slim, thick, or whatever your heart desires. You can have whatever you like," Lester voiced.

"Plus, all women don't do the same thing as other women and even if they do, some are better than others at certain things," commented Sylvester.

The two gentlemen gave one another a fist bump when Sylvester made his comment. I didn't see what was so profound about what he said, but they enjoyed it. I was just taking it all in. The lounge for me was a financial blessing as well as an educational treasure.

"Let's be honest; some women give better head than other women do. Some women have good pussy, but have terrible head, but there's a way around that," Sylvester stated.

"It damn sure is! I find myself circumventing the situation all of the damn time and it works for me. I kind of consider it like build a bear. I get exactly what I want," Lester voiced proudly before he sipped from his beer.

Basically, these two men are "Substituting" in the dating game. Substituting is when you plug in one thing for another. A man will have one woman who he dates or sleeps with who is good at one thing, but may be weak in another area. For example, he'll have one woman who his great in bed, but if she's weak when it comes to giving oral sex, he'll have another woman who is great at that. Also, he may have one woman who he deals with who is a great cook and another who is an absolute freak. Since most women are not great at all of those things, he substitutes them in and out as he sees fits. The bonus for him is that he never goes without the best of what he desires.

If you think about the concept of substituting as it pertains to sports, it's the exact same thing. A coach substitutes players in and out of games for many reasons. If a player is tired, the coach will give that player a break and put someone else in. Men often get tired of women and take a step back from them, so basically giving her a break. The man's "team" is comprised of women who all specialize in different areas, just like a basketball team. For example, one player may be a great scorer, another teammate is great at getting rebounds, while another teammate may be great at playing defense. The coach of the team uses them accordingly to make the best team possible. That's what men often do. Men will switch women in and out of their lives based on what they need at that moment in time. Through mixing and matching or "Substituting", men will build a complete woman.

Although I asked Sheena not to interrupt me, she still does. I'm not surprised though because her eyes have been getting bigger and bigger with every sentence I uttered. She finally bursts from containing herself for so long.

"Sage, it seems like you are trying to tell me that with all the females you came across at the lounge and at Howard that you weren't dibbling and dabbling. I know that's bullshit, so don't act like it's not. Hell, that's the reason why we broke up in the first place according to you," Sheena injects.

"Now, you agreed not to interrupt, but that clearly isn't the case. I'm not saying that at all, so calm down. If you let me explain and not cut me off, you'll get to what I'm saying," I shoot back quickly.

"Damn, you're right. My bad, I won't cut you off anymore... At least, I'll try not to, but I just had to make sure you weren't being a hypocrite. Like you were going to condemn those men for what they were doing as if you were better than them. You know I'll check you or anyone else if need be," Sheena voices assertively.

I reply, "Sheena, I'm sure you'll cut me off again because it's just in you to express yourself, but please try not to. Damn, you made me forget where I was."

"You were talking about the men at the lounge and "Substituting," Sheena states.

"That's right. I'm not saying that I'm better than them, but the guys at the lounge that day were in committed relationships, so they were running game on those women. They were breaking their trust. I tried my best not to be tempted by the countless attempts of the women at the lounge, but I wasn't always successful. I had some nights that I wish I could take back," I say.

"Like what?" Sheena asks.

"See, I knew you were going to interrupt again. You just can't help yourself. Besides, you don't want to know. I promise you. It's all old news and really does you no good to know, so I don't see the point," I reply.

"Sage, I'm not a little girl. You're my man and our relationship is strong, so it can't hurt me. I know you have a past just like I do. It's cool and I like juicy stories anyway," Sheena offers.

I give in to Sheena's request and tell her what she wants to hear. She's right that I have a past and she still accepts me. Her stomach is better than mine because I don't care to hear about her past. I'd rather not hear about who she had sex with or anything of the sort.

I remember one of many times when things got very sticky at the lounge. It was a Friday night after Thanksgiving. I'll never forget it in a million years. I decided not to go back to Linden for the holiday break from school because I was so focused in on the lounge. Surprisingly, the weather was warm for a late November day, so the lounge was bustling that night. While I was at the bar serving drinks, a girl named Alexis walked in. I had a class with her and she had been to the lounge before, so it wasn't a big deal. I was actually glad to see her because I wanted to hit that for a long time, but couldn't get my hands on her.

"Hey, big head," Alexis greeted as she sat at

the bar.

"Damn, I guess my secret isn't safe. I see the word got out about how big my head is. I should have known that it was only a matter of time," I remarked sarcastically.

Alexis laughed, while she responded, "Sage, you're crazy as hell. I can't with you... I can't. Give me a drink. I want an Incredible Hulk."

"I got you. I'm shocked that you're still in town. I figured you'd head back to Denver for the holiday to be with your family," I voiced.

"Trust me, I wanted to go, but I didn't have the money or the time to head back, so I stayed put. That flight was a little too much for me to stomach. I'm not getting money like you are. It's cool because I'll go home for Christmas break," Alexis told.

"I totally feel you on that. You would've spent a lot of money to go home now and then drop the same bread to go back in roughly two or three weeks for the winter break. I woulda stayed too. I'm doing alright for myself, but I ain't balling like that though," I verbalized.

"Right, that woulda been like twelve hundred dollars in total. Shit, my credit cards are already hemorrhaging... And Sage, stop it because everybody knows that you're eating heavy from here. I saw your new whip and I know it wasn't cheap," Alexis spoke.

We chatted on and off for about an hour while I served other customers. She was just as cool and bubbly as she was on campus. She tried on several occasions to buy her own drinks, but I wouldn't let her. She asked me why I didn't leave for the break and I explained to her that I had to work. The crowd unusually subsided for a while that night, so I just stayed at the bar conversing with Alexis until she was ready to go.

"Alright, let me get my ass outta here. I've been in here way too long. I only came to check to see if you were here and get one or two drinks," uttered Alexis.

I replied, "True. Well, it was good kicking it with you. I'll see you next week in class. Word up, I'm glad you stopped in."

"Yeah, me too. It was good seeing you too. I'll be in class in the back seat like normal. You know I don't be feeling sitting up front," Alexis said. "Thanks for the drinks too. I got you next time though."

"It's nothing. You're good people, even though you were talking behind my back about my big head. Keep my big head out ya mouth," I responded hoping to get a specific response.

My slick and low-key sexual comment landed exactly where I wanted it to. Alexis wasn't the least bit dimwitted, so she picked up on my comment as soon as I said it. She was a straightforward girl and was very confident. I figured if she heard about my big head that she may be somewhat interested in it. Also, why would she come to the lounge to check me out if she wasn't looking for something? I knew she didn't come to the lounge for nothing and she didn't.

Alexis replied sharply, "I never had ya big head in my mouth and for all you know, I might not want it in my mouth. Sage, I know one thing that's for sure... if I did have ya big head in my mouth, you would never in ya life tell me to keep it outta my mouth."

Alexis looked me straight in my face when she said that. There was no backing down now and I could tell she was just waiting for my response. I had to respond with something that was commensurate with her comment to me. I lived for this sort of thing. Battle of the wits type of conversations were my thing. It was almost like she was challenging me. I thought for a second that she may just be teasing me, but I had to find out for sure. Scared money don't make money is all I know.

I shot back, "Talking slick while you're walking away isn't exactly fair. You're talking like you're about that action while you're going the other direction. My big head might want to see if you're as good as you claim you are."

"I'm not running and my mouth is far better than I could ever describe. Have your toes curling like Eddie Murphy's did in '*Boomerang*' or have you sprung like Sunshine did the white guy in '*Harlem Nights*'. There's no need for me to sit in here with you all night while you're working. It's not like we can get it popping now, so I'm outta here," Alexis orated.

She was correct about me not being able to leave the lounge, but she didn't know about my room in the back. I knew I could find out real soon if she was pump faking or if she was serious about her trash talking. I had a ruse that would enable me to learn if she was a dick tease or the real deal.

"If you want to get it in, we can right now. That's not a problem because I can make that happen fairly easily," I boasted.

She stated, "Nah, it's cool because if you leave and get fired, you'll be blaming me for it. I don't need or want that on my conscience and I'm not meeting you in your car to suck ya dick there. We'll link up another time."

I remarked, "That's that bullshit right there. It sounds like you're scared to me, but I don't have to leave and I'm not talking about no in the car shit either."

Surprisingly, Alexis wanted to hear what I had in mind. I told her that she could come to my room in the back to chill for a little bit. She informed that she was fine with that. The only problem was that the back rooms were strictly off limits to customers. Normally, I wouldn't have cared, but there were some employees working who most likely would have told Mrs. Kline about me having a female in the back. I didn't want that conversation to even take place, so I came up with something that would prevent all of that.

Allowing a person, especially a female, to leave the lounge intoxicated was highly frowned upon by Mrs. Kline because of the legal and financial ramifications behind it, so I played that to my favor. All of the staff had seen Alexis drinking for the last few hours, so they wouldn't think it was strange for her to be drunk. Even though she wasn't even close to being drunk, the staff would have no way of knowing that. For that reason, I told Alexis to stumble around as if she were drunk and to slur her words.

She did exactly that and faked drunk to perfection. If I didn't know better myself, I would have thought she was wasted. She easily convinced the staff that she was out of it and in no shape to leave the lounge. The first staff member to attend to her fictitious drunken stupor asked me what he should do about her. I told him that we couldn't allow her to leave by herself and that we should take her to my room to let her sleep the alcohol off.

The guy complied with my decision and we carried Alexis to the back room. On the way to the room, I asked her if she had anyone we could call to come get her; just to convince the guy even further. She responded in an unintelligible slur. She was too good at playing the part and I hoped that she was just as good if not better at sucking my dick. Both men and women seem to have an affliction for over stating their sexual abilities.

The funniest thing in the world to me is that I always hear people report how bad someone else's sex is, but I never hear that person talking about how bad their own sex game is. Someone out here is really being dishonest.

We took Alexis to the back room and rested her on my bed. After getting her settled, me and the staff member walked back into the lounge. He resumed his normal duties and I told another bartender that I had to leave out for a minute and would be right back. I made sure the guy who helped me with Alexis saw me leave out the front door. I walked out the front door and went around the lounge and let myself in through the back door. The short corridor allowed me to go back into my room without being detected.

I walked into my room and noticed that all of Alexis' clothes were folded up on my couch. She was under the covers ass naked. My dick got rock solid and became uncomfortable in my clothes, so I did the only natural thing and stripped. When I disrobed, Alexis's mouth dropped.

"Damn, you really do have a big head!" Alexis stated with excitement.

I confidently stated, "I don't be bullshitting! My shit thick and long!"

I walked over to the bed and yanked the comforter off of it. Her flawless body laid there naked. Her pussy was freshly shaven and looked unblemished. I walked right over to her without saying a word and stuck my dick in her mouth. She opened her mouth as wide as she could and tried to swallow my entire dick, but she couldn't. My dick was too big and wouldn't fit. I have a big ego to say the least. She sucked my dick with the skill and precision that she boasted about previously. Her mouth was hot and extremely wet, almost like a pussy would be.

I pulled my dick out of her mouth and told her to lie flat on her back and open her mouth very wide. I climbed over Alexis' face like I was going to do a pushup. As I hovered over her in push up position, I lowered by dick into her mouth slowly. I pumped her mouth with short strokes, so the head of my dick would be stimulated. Alexis reached up and even surprised me with what she did. She reached around my waist and pulled me down forcefully. My dick went all the way to the back of her throat and she just held me in that position and started swirling her tongue. Her eyes began to bulge out of her eyes while she slightly gagged on my dick. She released her grip from around my waist and pushed me up. My dick slid out of her mouth as glibly as it entered. She grabbed by dick at its base and spit on it and then started slurping it again.

I stopped getting my dick sucked and lied down behind her while we were on our sides. I lifted her top leg up and inserted my dick in her pussy. She squeezed and licked her nipples as I stroked her pussy. She moaned louder and louder with each stroke. I didn't want her to make too much noise, so I never gave her the full length of my dick. She twirled her lower half in sync with the pokes of my dick. Our bodies were both covered with a mist of perspiration as we were interwoven.

I decided to stick my dick a little further into Alexis' pussy. She didn't expect it and her entire body tensed up. She reached back and put her hand on my waist to prevent me from going that deeply again. I wanted to feel more of that pussy, so I went deeper and deeper with each of my next strokes. Alexis began to scream.

"Fuck! You're fucking me good baby! Oh, it's deep!" she exclaimed.

I began grunting as I felt the sensation to nut building up from my toes. I stopped caring about if anyone heard us fucking because I was chasing a nut and I knew it was gonna be massive. Each stroke of my dick to her pussy became a thunderbolt. I felt like I was dropping continuous bombs on her because she was screaming so incessantly. I firmly gripped her waist and ass to keep her from running from the dick. I pulled her to me as I banged her coochie with my dick. Alexis was flopping around like a rag doll as I gave her all I had. Seconds later I was about to nut, so I whipped my dick out of her pussy and started shooting a load of nut on her ass. Alexis turned around and put my dick in her mouth to suck out the rest of the nut.

Unfortunately, Sheena jumps back in and interrupts the story again. I questioned if I should tell her all of this, but she wanted full disclosure or at least she claimed she did. Everything I'm telling her is a part of the journey of how someone wanted to take her life. I've lied to her enough already and I am done lying.

"Sage, really? So, you just fuck everybody the same? You fucked her like you fuck me? That's how you're doing it?" Sheena asks angrily.

"Baby, cut it out. You're gonna get yourself worked up over nothing. You don't need to take it there. I'm not telling you this to open myself up to scrutiny or ridicule. I'm merely telling you what you asked me to pertaining to the plot against us," I suggest.

Sheena speaks, "I'm not worked up! I just asked a question and you're not trying to answer the question. It's all related to how we ended up where we are today. You can't say it's not, so answer the damn question Sage."

"You surely seemed worked up to me, but okay, I'll answer the question. Yes, the truth is that I fucked her the same way that I fuck you. I pounded her and everything just like I do you. The act of sex was the same physically," I assert.

"I can't believe you just admitted that. That's real fucked up. I just can't believe you sometimes," Sheena commented angrily.

"I hope you aren't mad, but you asked and I

answered. The truth is sex from person to person is physically the same, but that doesn't mean that it has the same significance. Sex is insert, stroke, and nut. You pretty much can't change it from person to person, but it is different based on how you feel about a person. When you and I have sex, we make love. It's physical, emotional, and mental. That's why sex with you is so amazing. With those other women it was all physical and I was totally detached," I narrate sincerely.

Sheena listens to my explanation and it eases her ill feeling toward me. She knows that there is an element of truth to what I said because she has had sex with guys where it was only physical and totally bereft of an emotional connection. I further explain that it's like playing a game of basketball at the park with friends versus playing for an NBA Championship. The act of shooting baskets and playing defense is all the same, but the two games themselves have totally different levels of significance. Sheena apologizes for getting mad at me and asks me what happens next with Alexis.

After we finished our sexual encounter, we both cleaned up. I exited the lounge through the back door and walked around to the front of the lounge and went back inside. Fortunately, nobody realized what I had done. The lounge was packed by the time I walked back in. I had only fucked Alexis for a half hour to forty-five minutes and the crowd had swelled. I immediately jumped into the chaos of handling the packed crowd. I was back at the bar serving drinks when I saw Liz on the dance floor. I wasn't surprised that Liz lived on the dance floor because that was a mainstay for her when she was in the lounge. She was Mrs. Party All The Time.

Liz and I weren't in a committed relationship, but we had chilled and fucked several times since she performed oral sex on me behind the bar. Liz was territorial in my estimation of her personality. She was a real firecracker too. I could never really determine how she would act from day to day. She was the type of woman whose mood could and would change in an instant. Even though Liz was moody, she was always ready to please me and I wanted to fuck her. For that reason, I was glad to see her in the lounge.

As planned, about fifteen minutes later, Alexis resurfaced from my room. She waved at me as she walked past the bar and headed for the exit. I subtly waved back at her and then started helping customers. I had fun with her, but didn't care to see her again anytime soon. I walked away from the bar to replace a bottle of liquor that had run out. I made it back to the bar a few minutes later and was handsomely confused.

What the hell is she still in here doing here? She was headed for the door when I went to get the bottle of liquor, but when I returned, Alexis was sitting at the bar like she was before we had sex. It didn't really matter why she was in there at that moment. All I knew was that she had to leave immediately. I tried to get her to leave by offering to call a cab for her, but she declined the offer.

Her declination told me that she was looking to stay for a while longer. I didn't want to ask a bunch of questions that would make it obvious to her that I wanted her to leave. Before long, Alexis revealed that one of her friends from school came in the lounge as she was leaving and asked her to stick around. Alexis took her up on her offer. That was cool, but why was she hovering around me at the bar? I didn't need her hanging around me at the bar and blowing up my spot.

I didn't know how she might act if Liz said something sideways to her, but what I did know was that I couldn't be the cause of any drama at the lounge. Unfortunately, I noticed Liz looking over at me talking to Alexis on two separate occasions. I knew at one point she would assume that I was trying to holler at Alexis and would come over to the bar to intervene. I decided to walk away from the bar in order to reduce the likelihood that crazy Liz would approach. I took a bottle of champagne to a table of customers.

Liz approached me as I was delivering the champagne. As I figured, she was upset about Alexis being at the bar with me. I played dumb like it wasn't what it was, but Liz wasn't buying my story. Liz told me that she was just going to ask Alexis what the deal was herself. She walked away from me and headed over to the bar to confront Alexis. I walked behind her to keep her from grabbing Alexis if she attempted to, but good favor was on my side because Alexis was nowhere to be found. Maybe she decided to leave. I really didn't know.

Liz stated sternly, "Don't let me find ya lil friend back over here in your face. Sage, I'm not stupid! I know you well enough to know that you either fucked her or are gonna fuck her. I'm not telling you who you can and can't fuck, but I'm not gonna let her be all in your face while I'm in here."

Liz was definitely bugging, so I walked away without entertaining her any further. I had plenty of work to do and was not going to be distracted. The bar was getting slammed, so I went back over to help alleviate the swelling. Twenty minutes after returning to the bar, Alexis and her friend popped back up. I immediately looked around to see if Liz was watching me. I saw Liz watching me like how a hawk locks in on its prey. When Liz and I made eye contact, she started shaking her head from side to side in disapproval of Alexis being back at the bar.

Normally, I would just tell her to calm down and that our relationship was just casual, but I couldn't risk her acting violently in the spot.

Next, she tapped her wrist as to indicate that the clock was ticking for me to get rid of Alexis. I tried to shoo Alexis and her friend away, but I couldn't. They were locked in and weren't budging. Liz got out of her seat and began heading in our direction. Damn, Liz was going to do some off the wall shit.

The lounge was mobbed with people, so Liz couldn't make it to us as fast as she would have liked. I walked to the other side of the bar and gave Alexis a hug and squeezed her booty. With the place being so packed, no one really noticed anything. By the time Liz got to the bar, Alexis and her friend were gone. Liz told me that Alexis got lucky because she was going to drag her through the lounge. I believed her too because that was her temperament.

A little while later, my phone started ringing over and over again. It was Alexis and she wouldn't stop calling and texting me, but it was for good reason. I needed a ruse to get her out of the lounge to keep the peace. She had made mention of my nice car earlier, so I used that against her. I sent her outside so she could look at it, but what she didn't know was that she wouldn't be able to get back inside. When I went around the bar to give her a hug, her license was in her back pocket. I eased her license out of her pocket while I was groping her booty. We never allow anyone without identification to enter the club because it's the law. Her texts and phone calls were for me to come to the front to let her back in, but I never did. I just ignored all of the messages. I even went so far as to text the security at the front and informed them not to let her in no matter what she told them. She never did return and the night went on without any disturbances. It worked out perfectly and I was even able to fuck Liz that night.

Sheena interrupts again, "Sage, you were terrible back then. I'm glad you turned your life around. Well, the fucking everything moving part is all you turned around. Obviously, with what happened to Kevin, Eric, and the rest of them, you still have a scheming mind."

I respond, "Don't act like I was by myself in all of this! You were doing a lot of fucking and scheming too. I guess we're like two peas in a pod."

"That's right. And that's why you're my man! Don't forget it," Sheena boasts.

CHAPTER 5

The end of the month was always a hectic time at the club for me. One reason it was busy was because all of the bills were due. I had to make sure all of the vendors got paid for their supplies, no exceptions. Secondly, I had to order more things for the club. Lastly, all employees of the lounge who received monthly payouts had to be paid. Not to mention, we always had a heavy crowd toward the end of the month because people got paid around that time of the month. They normally had extra cash around then and wanted to ball out a little.

I remember back in the day, we could count on Mr. Kline like clockwork being at the lounge when it was pay day or a big event. He'd been collecting a check from the lounge for quite some time. At the end of a month, when he came to collect his check, he would order three drinks for himself and never paid for them or leave a tip for the bartender. That was Mr. Kline's personality because he was always thinking of himself. He despised the club, but didn't despise the money. What a hypocrite he was. He was the only person who collected a check from the lounge, but did absolutely no work. However, I was actually glad he wasn't around frequently. Since he was on the monthly expense payout list, he was still entitled to his cut of the profits. Without him starting the lounge, I never would have gotten into the business. His earnings had to be reported to the IRS by us, so he was listed as an employee. He had no problem throwing it in everybody's face and belittling what we did. He often let us know that he was the second highest paid employee behind Mrs. Kline, but he did no work. I guess that was his claim to fame. Getting paid to be completely removed from all hard work and decision making made him happy. That way of living was not for me. I like to work for the money I make.

It was the end of the month and of course Mr. Kline was here again with his hand out. I had his check in the back and ready to go, but I couldn't get free to go get it for him because there was a steady stream of customers and we were down one waiter and one bartender. Mr. Kline was fine with waiting because there were plenty of females at the lounge. He even made friends with Carol, who was a regular. Carol had come a long way since we first met.

Carol was married for six years and had two little girls and was riding high. Unfortunately, it all came crashing down on her. Her husband was cheating and she found out about it, but had no physical proof. To make matters worse, her husband was the sole provider for the family and was worth millions of dollars. When it came time to hire an attorney, she had no money to do so because her husband cleaned out all the accounts she had access to. She was in the lounge crying and drinking herself into a stupor. I wanted to help her, so I called in a favor and my lawyer James represented her for free upfront. He only took a portion of what she won in the divorce settlement. She eventually was awarded the house, a small fortune, and child and spousal support. By this time, Carol was living her best life. The crazy thing is that she still didn't work. She just spent her days caring for her girls. Carol became very assertive and spoke her mind. She gained strength from her divorce. She did all of the things she wanted to do while she was married, but couldn't. Since she was freed from her anchor, she traveled to almost every corner of the world.

Carol said, "You have been ordering drinks and food and haven't paid for anything."

Mr. Kline replied, "That's because I own this place."

"Sage, this gentleman says he owns the place.

Is that true?" Carol asked me.

I quickly stated, "Yes, he sure does. That's the truth."

"I wouldn't lie about such a thing. Why would I lie about owning a half ass night club?" Mr. Kline asked.

"Half ass! I love this place. It's fun, the drinks are the best in town, and the food is delicious. I would love to be a part of this organization. Me and my associates are always looking to invest and take on projects," said Carol.

"If you love it so much, you should buy me out. I'm sure we can come to an agreeable amount. I am looking to get out of the night club business and invest into other things, but the price has to be right," Mr. Kline spoke sternly.

Carol shot back, "Maybe I might."

"You just might like it," Mr. Kline uttered.

"I never thought about owning a lounge before, but you never know. Let's meet sometime next week and see what we can hammer out. We only invest in profitable business ventures," voiced Carol.

They exchanged business cards, so they could set up a meeting time. I was upset with Mr. Kline for discussing selling the lounge at the lounge. He had no respect for Mrs. Kline. Any person with dignity would have discussed selling the lounge somewhere else. He and Mrs. Kline built the lounge together and it meant nothing to him. It pained me and I was sure Mrs. Kline would feel the same way too. I guessed it was only normal that it was that way because they had never really saw eye to eye on anything in recent times. When Mrs. Kline thought right, Mr. Kline thought left. When he would scream hot, she would scream cold. Many people wondered how they were able to stay wed for as long as they did.

After speaking to Carol, Mr. Kline was in a good mood for the first time since I had known him. He was so happy that he left without his check. It was good to see him like that, but I was glad he left for the night because a paying customer deserved that seat. As soon as Mr. Kline left, another gentleman sat down in the vacant seat. The man ordered one shot of vodka and began turning around in his seat and peering around the lounge. I wondered if he is supposed to meet somebody or if he was casing the place.

"Excuse me sir. Are you looking for someone? I will help you if I can," I stated.

In a sly voice, he answered, "Yeah, yeah, I am looking for someone, but no one in particular and no I don't need your help. I'm looking for the woman I'm leaving with tonight. I'm sure you know what I mean."

"I know what you mean," I replied.

"Looks like it will be a good night for me because this place is packed. I am sure on nights like tonight, you'll take one home too," he uttered.

"Nah, it is all business for me. I get my kicks

out of making sure my customers are good and things run smoothly. That's the nature of customer service," I narrated.

"You must be blind because there is no way a seeing man is not swayed by all the beauty and curves these women have in here tonight!" he worded.

The level of excitement this guy possessed over the women in here reminded me of freshman year in college. The female freshman dorm was filled with girls who had not had much freedom while they were under their parent's roofs. They craved the attention of the male students on campus and guys knew it. The girls would sit out on the cement stoops in front of the dorms waiting for dudes to approach them. The guys on campus would put on their best clothes and head over to the dorm. I remember they used to be extra excited about the possibility of getting some. Their energy levels were turned all the way up. I always liked when things reminded me of undergrad. It was a great time and moment to be in. Even when I don't necessarily agree with the things that reminded me of times past, I still enjoy the mental trip through memory lane.

"I may be blind to certain things, but my vision is very clear when it comes to my future. I will not be blinded by temporary thrills and frivolous conquests," I suggested.

He arrogantly replied, "Get it how you live

because I am gonna get it how I live. It's time I run my game on these females. I got a fool proof process all worked out and it's a winner. I should bottle this game up and sell it. Works every time. I'd make millions."

I interrogated, "What do you have in mind?"

The man pulled out his phone, placed it on the bar, and tapped the screen. His phone was not illuminated, so I didn't get why he pulled it out as if he had revealed the key to solving a mystery. I looked at the phone and then he hit a button that made his screen light up. When the screen lit up, I saw a picture of what looked like a ten year old boy.

The guy stated, "This is the key to my success. This is really all I need to seal the deal."

"Is that your son?" I asked.

"Well, in real life he's not my son, but when I meet women, I tell them that the kid on my phone used to be my son," he answered.

"You're telling them that he *used* to be your son, meaning that he's no longer your son. Now, the only way that's possible is if the kid died or you dated the kid's mother and you assumed the role of his father, but you and the mother parted ways and now you can't see the boy anymore," I narrated.

"Right, that's exactly right. In most cases, I tell them that I dated the boy's mom and then we parted ways and she won't allow me to see him anymore. Furthermore, I'm having a hard time getting over it," he spoke.

I remember thinking that guy was a real piece of shit. I wasn't shocked that he was being deceptive because I've seen my share of unsavory men in here, but I was surprised that he was willing to use a kid as part of his ruse to get women. That was a first for me, but men operate on a whatever works type of mentality. A score is all that matters to them.

I say, "Sheena, the game he was running was called "The Seduction". I coined the phrase in one of my classes after we read an article about cheating men."

"Sage, you have a name for everything. I've never heard of that before, but I'm sure you won't hesitate to tell me what it is, so go ahead and tell me what it's about," Sheena speaks.

"You know I'm going to put you on to what he was doing," I state. "The guy put his phone on the bar top with his screen constantly illuminated. Even if you aren't a nosy person, you can't help, but see his phone screen. That's exactly what he hoped for and it worked. All night long, females came to the bar to order drinks and commented on his screensaver of the little boy. They asked the guy if that was his son and he responded accordingly. They told him how cute the boy was and how the kid must get his looks from his father. He was able to get many phone numbers from those conversations. He ended up getting exactly what he was looking for because one woman who was at In the Mix alone sat down to talk to and have drinks with him. I listened to him tell his story and she went for it. They eventually left together."

The Seduction worked for the guy. The Seduction is a game that men run where they entice a woman on a particular level in hopes to have sex with her. They may seek to reach you on a sexual level from the very beginning, but if not, they will try to entice women on an emotional level. The point is to draw the woman in any way possible to get them sexually. The guy's ploy is to play on the hearts of women because he knows that many women love children. He gives them that sob story about the boy on his screen to get the woman emotional. Once he pulls a woman in emotionally, he'll work on creating a shift away from the emotional connection. The next step of The Seduction is to create sexual tension between him and her. Ultimately, the encounter will end in the sexual tension being released by the two of them having sex. In many cases that's all the man wanted, so he'll disappear on the woman at some point. Often, the man will seduce the woman sexually from the very beginning if he feels he can. The emotional seduction is only implemented when he feels that has to use that method to get into a woman's good grace. Often times, men will introduce alcohol into the equation to lower a woman's defenses against his tactics. Since nothing is one hundred percent effective, the man will abandon ship if The Seduction doesn't work in a reasonable timeframe.

CHAPTER 6

After all of years of working at the lounge, there was always one thing that never ceased to amaze me. It was just one thing that I could never get my head around. Everybody who came to the lounge was always so free with their personal business. They told about affairs they had, they spoke of affairs they heard of, and even shared information about how much money they made at their jobs. I always wondered if it was the liquor they drank that made them so quick to drop such vital and private information. Then I thought some people just have a need to get things off their chests. Communication is therapy for many. Talking allows people to heal and relieve themselves of burdens they are carrying around.

Even though it serves as healing for many, I was never one to share my personal business. It seems like holding my personal business to myself is what makes sense. If people know someone's personal business, they can cause that person harm. The harm could be physical, emotional, or financial. Whatever the harm is, I don't have the least bit of time for it. I learned that a long time ago in high school. There was always drama stemming from people sharing other people's business. Many fights were started because students couldn't seem to tend to their own business. They never could figure out the solution to their issues. The solution was simple. Keep your business to yourself.

A lot of patrons to the lounge would ask a lot of questions about me. They would ask things like do I have any kids, am I married, or where do I live? I would find clever ways to get out of answering their questions. There was no need to be rude. None of my co-workers at the lounge knew my personal business. It was just better that they didn't know my situation. The staff members, however, all knew each other's business. They knew who was making what, who did what, and who was sleeping with whom. To make matters worse, they communicated the information back and forth like it was nothing. Some information is just not meant to be public.

In fact, I had to terminate an employee because of confidentiality violation issues. The employee was on the cleaning staff and was in my office performing her normal cleaning duties and then got curious. She decided to access financial records pertaining to the club. Her goal was to find out if the club could afford to give her a larger raise. She found the information she was looking for without anybody knowing. The next day, she communicated to her co-workers on the custodial team what she had done. Before the day was over, Mrs. Kline and I had been told what she had done and why. Mrs. Kline was very upset by the untrustworthiness of the employee.

She called a meeting for all of the employees of the lounge. She had chairs set up on the dance floor for all of us to sit in so she could address us all at once.

She said, "I brought all of you here today to inform you of some things. I am saddened that my word isn't enough to satisfy your concerns about the wages. I gave everyone a raise and explained to you that more was to come. I asked all of you to be patient with me while I make some very important business moves for the lounge. I like to think I have been generous to you during your tenure here. I find it disheartening to hear that people on staff have been dishonest. Sage, you can address the staff. I trust your judgment in resolving. It's up to your discretion."

Mrs. Kline waved goodbye to the staff and left the lounge. She had a look of dejection on her face. I could tell she was hurt by the situation. I was actually hurt and disappointed myself. I was not hurt because of the snooping of the staff member, but I was hurt because Mrs. Kline was hurt. She was always fair with me and the staff, so I couldn't understand why the staff member didn't believe her when she said another raise was forthcoming.

That was the only time I ever had to address the entire staff when it wasn't a big day for the lounge such as New Year's Eve or Halloween. I definitely never had to address the staff as a whole for something of that nature. I felt awkward and a bit embarrassed about having to address them. Most of them were great employees who never had to be reprimanded for anything. Unfortunately, one bad apple can cause the whole group to suffer. It also makes for a tense situation in the workplace and more work for everyone involved. I addressed the work group.

I said, "I am disappointed to have to address the group on these terms. I want to stress the importance of tending to your own affairs and being where you are required to be. It is important to our success in the lounge. We can't operate effectively without it."

After a few words with the staff, I dismissed the meeting. I also pulled the employee who was snooping into my office. I didn't want to address her in front of the entire work group because it may have caused a scene. Unfortunately, she could no longer work at the club, so I fired her.

A lot of old memories flashed through my mind one night at the lounge, while I listened to several conversations simultaneously. One girl named Dana was talking about how her boyfriend was so disconnected. She was carrying on and on, but then said he wasn't disconnected from reality or from her. As she continued to talk, what shocked me was what he was disconnected from.

"Girl, he is so disconnected. He doesn't have any social media. No Twitter, no Instagram, no nothing!" Ebony said.

Her friend replied, "What? Are you serious? How could he not have anything?"

Ebony stated, "I know right. That's what I'm saying. Who isn't on social media by now? We are in the age of technology for God's sake."

"Sage, why do you think a guy wouldn't have social media?" Dana asked.

"Maybe he is too old and feels it is something for the younger generation. His age matters," I replied.

"He is only 22 and is pretty involved in the latest fashion. I don't see what would keep him from getting into the fad. It would be nothing to jump on the social media bandwagon," Dana stated.

I asked, "What are two reasons why you are on social media?"

Dana quickly responded, "I'm on it to see what everybody is doing and also because I want to keep in contact with my friends."

"I am sure you can keep up with your friends without social media. All you have to do is text or call them. As for as seeing what everybody is doing, that's just being nosy," I voiced.

Dana uttered, "You're right about both of those, but I wanna know about him.

I asked, "Have you ever heard of 'The Discretion' scheme?"

"No, what the hell is that?" she asked.

I explained that "The Discretion" is a scheme that dudes run all the time. This form of deception involves a guy being very discreet. He will try to not meet any of your friends or family. He will really try to only deal with you. "The Discretion" calls for him to be very systemic in his movements. He will be very cautious in the things that he says and does. He may not take many pictures or take you to public places because he's trying to be secretive.

Now let's add social media into the equation. Social media is designed to connect people with other people. They share all sorts of information on those sites. They all serve a valuable purpose and are necessary to many people for entertainment or business purposes. Social media is the antithesis of "The Discretion". The two are like Batman and the Joker. They are the same as good versus evil and protagonist versus antagonist. The point of the guy not having social media is because he is trying to operate under low exposure. If he is linked into social media, he will be giving up his cover. Social media will allow everyone to be linked into his personal business. That is something he is not trying to do. It makes it too easy for everyone to know his business and potentially tell on him, if he is not doing the right thing.

"Wow! That does make a lot of sense. I am gonna check him on that first chance I get," she exclaimed.

"You never know. He could just think social media is dangerous and doesn't want to fall victim to any scams or other illegal activity," I reported. "Let's be real... Identity theft is happening as we speak and he may be fearful of that."

The two of them did not finish their drinks and left immediately. They seemed to be on a serious mission. I hoped I didn't get anybody in trouble unnecessarily because my intent was only to help.

I remember that day vividly because Jasmine left for Europe and she was happy out of this world. She was smiling from ear to ear and even gloating a little bit. It was cool with me. She spoke about the endless opportunities that awaited her. Hope is a beautiful thing and she had plenty of it.

I was also happy for Jasmine's good fortune. Unfortunately, everybody did not feel the same way I did. Mrs. Kline totally disapproved of her leaving. She was upset she was not a part of the decision Jasmine made to accept the job. Her mom was not going to sleep well while she was gone. Mrs. Kline was always protective of Jasmine. Jasmine's an only child and has always been approached by all sorts of guys. As a mother, Mrs. Kline just wanted to protect her child from this cruel world. However, Mr. Kline was indifferent about the situation. He felt like it was time for her to live her own life and make her own decisions. He didn't try to keep her from going or encourage her to go. He didn't care because it didn't impact him financially and that's all that mattered to him those days.

After we took Jasmine to the airport, Mrs. Kline and I drove back to the lounge to discuss a few items. We ate lunch and talked about Jasmine and old memories for a while. Mrs. Kline eventually switched the conversation to what was really on her mind.

"Sage, remember when I mentioned to you I was considering opening another In the Mix?" she asked.

I replied, "Yes, it was some time around Halloween. The day after, if my memory serves me correctly. You said there were some pros and cons to the move."

"Such a sound mind you have. The benefits of youth. I can't believe you remember that so clearly. Enjoy it while it lasts," Mrs. Kline said.

I smiled as she continued with what she

wanted to share. I've always had a pretty sharp mind and I think it's very important to have one. I pride myself in being fortified and driven, so it meant a lot to me when she complimented me on my mindset.

"I told you that night that I would make a decision and I have done so. I will not be opening another location. I feel the current state of the lounge is fine. We are experiencing growth and I think it is best we keep it that way. Many times when small businesses expand, they lose their genuine nature. I am afraid In the Mix will become too trendy and commercialized. That generally leads to being driven by numbers and profits and not by doing what's right. I know the detriments far outweigh the benefits," she narrated. "Not to mention, I'm older in age now and don't need the extra stress."

"I understand where you are coming from. I have heard of many small businesses being corrupted by the demands of becoming too big. Things are great the way they are," I said.

Mrs. Kline replied, "I am glad you understand. I thought you might be disappointed about the news because you were excited when I initially told you what I was considering."

I verbalized frankly, "Overall, I am in a great position. I can't complain about anything. It's your decision and I support you. If expanding doesn't work for you, then don't do it. It is really just that simple."

I did have one question for her that mattered a great deal to me. I figured I would ask just to get it off of my chest. The last thing I wanted to do was go forward without knowing things that could directly impact me.

I asked, "How does this impact my three percent of ownership?"

She replied, "That is a great question. You don't have to worry about that. Your three percent is protected as long as you are an employee of the lounge. You can relax, if that's what you're worried about. Again, this is something that's between me and you. Sage, your financial matters between us are nobody's business. Confidentiality is vital to any good business proceedings."

I am glad she said that. I felt bad about not telling her about how Jasmine got the funds to move to Europe. Fortunately, she felt that discretion was key and that sometimes you have to use your judgment when it comes to sharing information. Jasmine and I agreed to only tell Mrs. Kline when the time was right. If Mrs. Kline felt our agreement was worthy of discretion then clearly the pact Jasmine and I made was worthy of the same. Besides, it really didn't matter how she got the money at that point because she was gone.

CHAPTER 7

My thoughts about whether I should inform Mrs. Kline were definitely mixed. I was vacillating between telling her and not telling her. I was experiencing internal conflict because I didn't want to be considered a liar and a cheater. She did say that business was not to be discussed openly. The million-dollar question is if withholding information is lying? Is it cheating if you haven't done anything dishonest, but you know something that another person may want to know? If someone wants to know something, isn't it their responsibility to ask the question?

We had a discussion in one of my classes that actually turned from discussion to a heated argument over the idea of cheating. The professor proposed a series of questions and we had to free write about them. We had five minutes to write down whatever came to mind for each question.

He first asked, "What is cheating?"

That question alone sparked interest in the entire class because we all were sure the right answer rested with us. There was chatter among my classmates before we even had time to answer the question.

After five minutes, he asked, "Does everyone cheat?"

"All men cheat! They are all dogs," yelled a classmate.

Some of the guys in the class did not take that comment lightly. They thought they were being targeted and stereotyped.

A male student responded, "It's not all of us! Make sure you have your facts straight before you make generalized statements!"

"Alright students. Be sure to always respect yourself and others while you are in the confines of my classroom. Disrespect will not be tolerated," said the professor.

The next question came after he gave his brief speech.

"Is all cheating the same?" he asked.

Every question had us writing miniature books because these are highly discussed topics. There were a plethora of answers that were at both ends of the spectrum. Once I got started writing, I couldn't stop. I couldn't wait to answer the question out loud. I hoped he would recognize me waving my hand like I was a little boy who had just seen his favorite basketball player. About twenty minutes later, I heard my name.

"Mr. McMillian, what is your position on the questions I posed?" he asked.

"I am going to read from my paper because I have a lot to say," I said.

He shot back, "No worries. The floor is yours."

I conveyed, "Cheating has more than one level in its meaning. Cheating on a basic level pertains to being dishonest or deceitful. With that being said, anytime you behave in a deceitful or dishonest fashion you have cheated. If we follow this definition, then it is safe to say that everyone is a cheater. It does not make you a bad person, it just makes you human. Part of our flaws as humans is that we are imperfect, full of sin, and we cheat. This type of "cheating" is synonymous to a little white lie. The little white lie that is told is almost accepted as being okay by people because it wasn't that big of a falsehood. Also, cheating on its most basic level can be looked at like driving a car. For example, the speed limit on the highway is posted at 60 miles per hour. However, there are many people who are not adhering to the posted speed limit. Some people are doing 65 miles per hour. They are doing just enough to benefit from going over the posted speed limit, but not quite enough to make a police officer want to pull them over. Technically, you are speeding because one mile over is a violation, but it is acceptable in today's society. Cheating on a basic level is what everybody does, so it's not seen as egregious, but it doesn't exclude people from being a cheater.

There is a surface level of cheating that everyone is apt to commit, but there is also a deeper meaning of cheating. The cheating I am speaking of is the cheating that occurs in a committed dating relationship or marriage. Many people often mistake cheating or mislabel cheating because a person has more than one sexual partner. If a person is not committed to anyone, cheating cannot take place. One of the more in-depth levels of cheating is when one person in a committed relationship goes outside of the relationship to have particular needs met. Not only does the mate step outside the relationship for his or her desires to be satisfied, the person cheating does not inform their mate of what they are doing. That's what makes it cheating. For example, if a man's wife approves of him sleeping with other women, he's not cheating. Cheating only can occur, if one party of the relationship is unaware of the other's actions.

It seems like most people associate cheating with having sex outside the relationship without their mate's knowledge. That certainly is cheating. This is a physical form of cheating that many people find offensive and completely unacceptable. Cheating is not only relegated to sex. Cheating can also be in the form of emotional gratification. I have a friend who was in a committed dating relationship with a guy who was very sensitive to her needs. According to her, the guy she was dating was not very sensitive. He was hard on the inside and out. There were times when she needed him to be emotionally available for her, but he wasn't because it just wasn't him. She decided to get a male friend who would support her emotional side. He would hold her and provide her comforting words when she needed them. Unfortunately, she did this without the consent or knowledge of the guy she was currently dating. In that instance, cheating has occurred.

A person can also cheat on their mate if he or she seeks and finds an outside person to communicate with. For instance, if your mate is a poor communicator and you covet a person who communicates well and you decide to find a friend who is what you are looking for, you have just cheated. What makes it cheating is that you have found someone outside of your relationship to meet your needs without confiding in your mate. This can be just as harmful to a relationship as sexual misconduct.

Lastly, cheating can occur on a financial level. Let's be honest, times are hard all over the place and sometimes a little supplement to the pocket book or wallet is just what the bills ordered. If you find yourself financially strapped and you receive aid from an outside source, you are guilty of cheating, if your mate has not given the all clear. It makes the situation worse when your mate asks where the extra income is coming from and you are misleading with your responses.

These are just three examples of the more in-depth levels of cheating. Again, if you step outside of your relationship to have needs met, you are cheating. Cheating is not just about sex. It's about being selfish and reckless. It's selfish because you are only considering yourself and what you want. It is reckless because you are jeopardizing your relationship. Cheating is also inconsiderate because you are not considering the feelings of your mate."

We certainly have had our share of cheaters come through the lounge over the years. We have even had to have people removed from the premises due to escalations inside our place of business. It seems that most of the drama we've encountered over the years has fallen on Valentine's Day.

One Valentine's Day celebration is the most memorable of them all. That year Valentine's Day fell on a Saturday and naturally it was a busy night. Adding the fact that it was the day known for lovers and couples into the equation, made for a highly trafficked night at the lounge. We also added an extra incentive to come to In the Mix that night. I decided that it would be good for business that we offer two for one drinks that night. It seemed to be a clever way to get people to come out. The only requirement to get the buy one get one free drink special is to be with your significant other. It played perfectly into the whole concept of Valentine's Day. The sense of togetherness and unity was already palpable just in the spirit of the occasion. We went the extra mile to make our customers see that we really appreciated and encouraged the bond couples had.

The plan worked better than I anticipated. We had more people in the lounge that year than any other years prior. I was shocked to see my brother Dave there that night. He definitely played his part to make the night interesting. We always hoped to foster positive relationship building in the lounge and we completely achieved our goal. The two for one drink promotion not only facilitated more couples to come out and indulge in adult beverages, it also made singles get more familiar with one another also. Once the single people knew they had to be coupled up in order to get the drink special, they began aggressively talking to one another. Everyone was approaching everyone. Many relationships and connections were started that night and was credited to alcohol.

Unfortunately, it was not totally smooth sailing for everyone there. In a perfect world, everyone would do as they should, but the world is imperfect. People always seem to want to travel down the highway of deceit and that night was no different. Many dudes were living foul. They arrived at the lounge with women who were not their wives, girlfriends, or significant other. This made for a very precarious night for the guys who were creeping. It's very hard to creep at a place that has many people of various age ranges in it. It just becomes highly likely that you will run into somebody you know.

Marcus, who was a regular customer at the time, was in the lounge that night just like he was on any other big day. However, this Valentine's Day was very different from previous Valentine's Days. It was different because Marcus came alone. I thought this action was very strange because he was married and they were not estranged. They had just been in the club a few days ago. Not only did he not show up with his wife, he eventually linked up with another woman.

Sheena interrupts, "Not Marcus, Marcus! Damn, he was up to no good even back in the day. I see his ass been trifling!"

I answer, "Yeah, Marcus, Marcus. God rest his soul. He had been up to no good for a long time. Let me tell you what happened though."

"Yeah, tell me what happened!" Sheena voices emphatically.

The entire staff of bartenders and waitresses knew him by name and they also knew his wife on a first name basis. Once the staff noticed what was going on, they started giving each other looks. Eventually, the staff members were texting back and forth about how foul he was for doing what he was doing. One employee posted a comment to her Twitter account that stated 'So sad when you see dudes creeping on Valentine's Day". Twitter was in an uproar about her post and everyone had an opinion. I re-tweeted the following statement: "Ladies, if you are not with your man today, you need to really reevaluate your relationship status with him." That comment really sparked a Twitter-storm. However, that storm in cyber space was merely a drop of rain compared to the tsunami that flooded the lounge that night.

The lounge was loud and bustling all night, but the energy was raised exponentially when Marcus's wife showed up unexpectedly at the lounge. Her presence was known almost immediately when she entered the door.

"Where is my fucking husband? I know he is in here!" she screamed.

None of the staff who heard her dared to answer her question. They were too scared that somehow, they might become a part of the drama. They just continued serving the other customers without getting involved. I knew one of them had found a way to tip her off. If one of them didn't tip her off, it was somebody at the lounge that night. I could tell because of what she said.

"People sending me tweets about my husband

being in here with some bitch! Sage, I know you know where he's at!" she hollered.

I wanted to stay neutral in the situation, but I couldn't. I let her know I saw him and that was that. I am glad I didn't say that I hadn't see him because someone had already told her that her husband was at the bar ordering a drink from me and took a picture of him.

Marcus's wife asked, "Well, when you saw him, was he with another female?"

"When I served him the drink he'd purchased, there were many females around," I told her.

I didn't go any further with my narration and really hoped I did not have to. I knew I didn't quite answer the question appropriately, but I gave her just enough to assume I did. I didn't lie, but I didn't tell the whole truth.

As part of my studies at the university, I took a class on ethics. The class often entailed writing papers or having discussions on a multitude of topics. Telling lies was a topic we debated during one class session. When faced with lying to Marcus's wife, I was immediately taken back to that day in class.

When we got settled in the class, the professor asked a student to turn off the lights because we were about to watch a short video. The video served as the basis for the class discussion that day. In the video, a girl was given permission by her mother to attend a party. The party was over at 12:30 a.m. and the girl was given strict instructions to be home by 1 a.m. The girl went to the party and had the best time ever. She even returned home from the party by the time her mother told her to be. When she returned home, her mother was half asleep. The girl walked into her mom's room to inform her that she was home. Her mom acknowledged her daughter's presence and fell into a deep slumber.

The daughter left her mother's room and walked into her bedroom. Shortly after she reached her room, she received a text telling her that all of her friends were still hanging out and she should come back outside to join them. She wanted to go because it was always fun hanging with her friends. She assessed her situation and determined that she wouldn't get caught because her mom was a very heavy sleeper. The girl quickly changed clothes and stealthily snuck out of the house to hang out with her friends.

A few hours later the girl returned home. She did not know what to expect upon entering the house. She was fairly certain her mom wasn't up because she had not called or texted her. The girl walked into the house confidently, but her confidence was soon broken. Her mom woke up and summoned her to her room. Her mom noticed that her daughter was coming from the direction of the front door.

The mom said, "I know you didn't just get in here from that party! It's three thirty in the morning!"

The daughter quickly replied, "No mom. I am not just getting in from the party. I would never wear my bedroom clothes to a party."

Her mom realized that her daughter had on her bedroom clothes and that was not what she left the house in to attend the party. The video ends with the mom falling back asleep.

The professor instructed a student to turn the lights on again. There were a couple of questions on the board that stated, "Is omission of the truth, the same as lying"? "Was the girl lying to her mother?"

There were three sides to the yes or no question. Some people thought she was lying, some thought she wasn't lying, and others answered yes and no.

One classmate stated, "The daughter didn't lie because she answered her mother's question truthfully. She had not just returned from the party."

Another student agreed with her point of view. He felt like she did her job as a child and answered the question according to what her mom asked. He said it is not her job to provide information beyond what her mom asked. The class was in an uproar. Many people supported the girl's original statement, while others did not. The professor let the conversation continue without ever giving an official statement on what he felt. The professor always did things like that. He would let the class bounce ideas off one another and then leave the answer open-ended for the class to decide.

Marcus's wife was satisfied with my answer to her question and went looking for him. Unfortunately, I was not comfortable with my answer. My overall opinion about if withholding the entire truth is lying was seated in a person's intentions. Lying is making untruthful statements, but actually goes a bit further. For example, if a person withholds all of the truth and is doing this purposely, then he or she is lying. This is just a form of deception that makes people feel better about lying and gives them a justification for what they haven't admitted to. Another reason why I say I was lying is because I meant to be deceptive and misleading. I didn't want to spill the beans on the guy who was cheating, so I withheld the entire truth and sent her thinking down a different path. Anytime a person gains from withholding the entire truth, he or she is lying. In the case of the girl in the video from class, she was definitely lying. She knew her mom wasn't necessarily concerned with where she was coming from. Her mom was essentially concerned with what time she came in and if she made curfew. I hoped to gain something when I told Marcus's wife that he was standing near many females. I hoped to keep order in the lounge. I knew she would become violent or confrontational if she saw him with another woman. The lounge's future lies in my hands, so I knew I had to protect its integrity. However, I still had scruples about the situation. I decided to go find Marcus's wife to come clean about what I had done. Misleading her just didn't sit well with me. Unfortunately, I was too late.

Marcus's wife worked her way through the flock of people and approached her husband and his date.

She said, "This the bitch you in here wit! Boy, you downgraded!"

Marcus asked, "Babe, what you doing in here? When did…"

Before he could finish his sentence, she slapped him so hard she left her palm print on his face. He grabbed his face and started mumbling something with his hand over his face. The female he was with wasn't too happy about being called a bitch for no reason. She didn't even know Marcus was married. She attempted to express her disapproval, but that was short lived.

She stated, "I don't appreciate being called out of my name. You need to check yourself and your man. Don't be mad at me because you aren't woman enough to satisfy him and keep a happy home."

Marcus's wife stated, "Bitch, you just tried my life! I'm gonna handle him later at the house, but you real close to getting your ass whooped right now!"

"I ain't real close to shit, but having to get pulled up off your lil ass!" she screamed.

As she opened her mouth to utter another sentence, Marcus's wife slapped her in the face and grabbed her hair. The two females began punching and scratching each other. All of the female fights I've seen were always high energy. I knew better than to jump in and try to stop it. I figured I would wait for security to handle the situation. I just wanted to make sure the other patrons didn't get hit by anything. Marcus obviously didn't get the memo. He tried to grab his wife to stop the fight himself. Unfortunately, Marcus was wearing dress shoes that had zero traction. When he grabbed his wife, she jerked away from him and the thrust made him fall. Everybody knows that female fights can be very brutal and this one was no different. They eventually ended up on the floor rolling around screaming at each other and hitting whatever they could. The fight only lasted for about thirty seconds, but seemed like an eternity. The security team threw them out of the lounge right into the hands of the police. Things finally got back to order and the night continued without a hitch. Everyone had opinion about the dramatic occurrence, especially the guys.

"Yo, that dude is stupid. He actually came in here with his side chick! Don't he know better than that," said Jay.

"He has no game. It must be his first time cheating or something," said Barry.

Jay replied, "I know right. His wife comes in

here all the time and if she isn't, her friends are. She was actually a loyal wife. I tried to step to her and she shot me down because of him."

Barry stated, "He was never supposed to be here. He ain't even got any of his boys in here. Foolish! The best he could come up with was that lame line about it's not what you think. I kinda feel sorry for the guy."

The sad thing is that they missed the point too. They were more worried about his game being weak than they were at the fact that he was cheating. The real point is that he shouldn't have been cheating to begin with.

CHAPTER 8

Mr. Kline showed up at the lounge on a random day. It had been a while since he met with Carol to close the deal on him selling his portion of the lounge. He was only there to pick up the check he forgot to pick up the last time he was there. He sped out of the lounge that day with the quickness. However, he was a lot more friendly than normal. I guess it was because he was finally out of the club business. He was glowing like a woman who just got proposed to by her high school sweetheart. Apparently, Mr. Kline sold his ownership in the club for a handsome sum of money even though he could have gotten more if he was willing to wait and negotiate aggressively. He rushed the sale and process against the advice of his counsel because he wanted to invest in a once in a lifetime deal that Carol mentioned to him. I didn't blame him because when I want something, I go after it too. Since I met him, he's coveted a major investment opportunity. He was finally a part of what he desired. I love to see dreams come to fruition and it served as hope for me. Mr. Kline and I talked like we never had in the past.

"Sage, I am done! On to bigger and better things. Time for me to spend my golden years with the big wigs. Took a while, but I am on my way. With the money I made selling the lounge, I was able to make a strong power move," Mr. Kline said candidly.

"I am glad you've found what you are looking for. This has to be an exciting time for you. I know as I get older and things keep happening positively for me, I get excited," I worded.

Mr. Kline replied, "It's definitely an exciting time for me. Don't get bogged down in this place forever. You are better than working at a lounge doing bartending work. I've seen you around here for a while bartending and not progressing. It is time for a change. Leave now while you are still young."

I appreciated Mr. Kline's words. I knew I was better than bartending and wiping down tables, but he was wrong about me not progressing though. I had made many strides toward my dreams coming to fruition. I had money saved up and I had a strong clientele. Additionally, I had gained a multitude of connections during my time at the lounge. However, I didn't tell him any of that. No matter what I said, he wouldn't agree with it because he was against the lounge altogether.

"Thank you, sir. I appreciate the compliment. Maybe I can work for you when your new business venture gets off and running," I said.

"I'll definitely keep you in mind. I know you are trustworthy, determined, and profitable," Mr. Kline offered. "You were also always on time with my checks."

We both laughed and said our goodbyes. I figured I'd see him again because I didn't think he'd be able to resist the lounge. He was an older gentleman, but his thirst for pretty women in short skirts seemed to be too major in his life to completely just walk away. I liked the comments he made about me. The lounge was definitely making more money with me there. I compared the profits the lounge made before I was employed there against what it was making at that moment and there was a drastic difference. I was responsible for almost every aspect of the lounge. I was in charge of making sure the lounge's books were in order and everyone was paid accurately and on time. Mrs. Kline could do it, but she normally took longer and sometimes made mistakes with payroll. She had no problem letting me handle things because she trusted me and knew that business was flourishing. Each month, I gave her a report to show her what we made and what we spent.

RYAN HODGE

In the Mix was the hottest lounge in all of
D.C. We were in the running to be voted the
best nightlife spot in the district. Anytime there
was a concert, big sports game, or homecoming
event, we saw huge crowds. We were packed
almost every day of the week. Fridays and
Saturdays were always more crowded because
people flooded the streets to relieve some of the
stress of a long work week. We saw people from
a wide range of age groups on those days.
Sundays, Mondays, and Thursdays were days that
produced big turn outs because the National
Football League had games on those days.
Additionally, Thursday nights were college nights
at the lounge. We knew college students often
didn't have large sums of disposable cash, so we
had free admission and reduced drink prices for
anyone who had valid college credentials.

"I remember the college nights at the lounge.
We used to have so much fun there. Ilesha,
Rachel, and I were at the lounge all the time,"
Sheena blurts out.

I speak, "I remember. I used to see you and ya
girls on the dance floor, but could never get over
to you to make your acquaintance. I'll never
forget when you ended up at the bar that night
and I finally got to meet you. I had you on my
radar ever since then."

"Yeah, I remember that night clearly. I
remember everybody telling me that you were a
dog and that I shouldn't entertain you. I'm glad I

138

didn't listen to them. Plus, I figured they were wrong because when you said you were from Linden and I hadn't heard of you, my thoughts were that you were pretty low-key," Sheena reports.

"That's how I've always been...Under the radar and low-key. Not flashy or anything," I comment.

"Umm, I don't know about all that under the radar stuff you talking about, but you've admitted to fucking a lot of the women who have come through the club. I know you weren't fucking them while you were fucking me," Sheena utters emphatically.

"We've already been through this and you know I wasn't, so stop it. Once we became exclusive, I cut all of them off, but when we broke up, I resumed having a little fun," I explain. "I've never cheated on you."

"Ya ass better not have, but get back to the story of why someone tried to hurt me," Sheena shoots back.

In many instances, the football game watching crowd eventually mixed with the college crowd. There was no way to keep the two from meshing together. Often times, it made for a great night at the lounge. Unfortunately, men often took advantage of the situation. They came in to watch football, but eventually turned to making advances on the college aged women who were in there. It was like listening to a broken record when hearing different men speak. You would think they were reading from the same script. Many men who came to the lounge for game nights were professionals with plenty money to spend and used it to their advantage. Justin, who was a regular at the lounge on Thursdays, used to bring his friend to the lounge to partake in the night's festivities. I remember when they came pushing through the door one Thursday night. Justin and his friend immediately came to where I was and started asking me questions.

Justin asked, "Sage, what's going down? How you been?"

I replied, "Can't complain. Things are going according to plan."

"Good, good. This is my boy Brian. I'm trying to show him a good time tonight," Justin stated.

"Sage, nice to finally meet you. Heard a lot of good things about you," Brian said.

"That's what's up! Good meeting you as well," I stated. "You came to the right place if you're looking for a good night."

"It really looks like the place to be," Brian commented.

I fixed them their drinks and stepped away from the bar for a moment. When I returned moments later, Justin and Brian were watching the game and waiting for another round of drinks. I fixed them two more shots of Hennessey and made small talk with them.

"Who are you pulling for in the game," I asked.

"In tonight's game, I am pulling for myself," Brian retorted.

I said, "Oh, I see. You aren't here for the football game."

"Hell nah!! I'm here for these pretty young things in here tonight. Justin said they are easy targets. I'm trying to see if what he was talking about is official," explained Brian.

"Yeah, Sage, they are easy as taking candy from a baby. I am hitting something tonight or soon after," said Justin.

I was a bit disgusted to learn that these two guys were only in here to pick up on the young college girls. They were not man enough to pick up women who were formidable adversaries. I almost felt sorry for them. They really were pretty shallow and only had the mental capacity to engage girls barely out of high school.

"What's your approach?" I asked.

Brian questioned, "You want to use our game on them too huh?"

"No, I'm good on that. I don't run game merely for cheap thrills," I articulated.

Justin jumped in quickly and said, "We will just use their weaknesses against them. Simple as that."

Brian said, "They are all in here lacking something, so we will fill their void. Everybody wins! It's just a matter of finding out what their weaknesses are."

Fortunately, I was calm tempered because if I was not, I would have cursed them out and removed them from the lounge. Justin and Brian both had well thought out plans on what they were going to do. Justin only targeted females who were in college. He explained how they were perfect to target because college students were normally broke. He was in college before and remembered how many females didn't like to struggle. He planned to use their disapproval of struggling to his benefit. The girls would be inclined to give him what he wanted because they knew he would keep them from eating noodles and pop tarts.

Brian was no better than Justin. I saw why those two guys were in close council. They had the same mindset. Brian's plan was similar in nature. Brian had recently bought a new car and still had his old one. He knew that many females in college didn't have cars. Depending on their university, it was against university policy for freshmen to have cars. Also, many people didn't own a car because they simply couldn't afford it. He used this to his advantage. He would let females know he had two cars and would be willing to let them use it if they were with him. It was inconvenient for people to get around without a car. He knew that females needed to get to the grocery store, the mall, and other places and having a car made that process a lot easier.

He essentially was dangling bait in their faces and indirectly telling them what they have to do to get it.

That is a game that men run on women called "The Exploitation". This game is when men recognize areas where women are weak. The weaknesses can be anything from financial, emotional, or sexual in nature. Once the guy realizes the weakness the woman has, he will exploit her. During "The Exploitation" he will use her shortfalls or hardships to his advantage. In most cases, the man seeks sexual gratification. He will exploit the female for as long as he can. If she stops letting him exploit her, he will stop providing the favors he once was. In other instances, he may stop providing previous services rendered because he has moved on to another mark. It's also possible that the man will stop providing aid because he feels he has nothing else to gain by continuing "The Exploitation".

Anyone can be a victim of "The Exploitation". It doesn't matter what age you are. Men may target younger women because they tend to lack relationship savvy. They haven't had enough experience to combat an older man. What a younger woman may think is genuine, may be identified easily by an older more experienced woman as being fake. Another reason younger women may be singled out is because they are less established than older women. For example, a twenty-two year old is building her status and in most cases, needs more support than a woman who is thirty-two. The woman who is thirty-two, is likely to be autonomous and well established. Men know younger women are often in financial need, so they will use that to their favor. A man attempting to exploit a woman will dangle his money in her face knowing she is likely to grab the hook because she is in need. Also, younger females tend to be more materialistic than older women. This further plays into the favor of a man who seeks to exploit a woman. He can serve as the vehicle for her to get what she needs.

"Men are savages. I don't even see why women trust men. Y'all be doing the most just to get a little piece of ass. It just ain't that serious. Oh my goodness," Sheena remarks.

"Sheena, the game is real out here. That's why I used to try to school you so much about what is going on out here in these streets," I say.

CHAPTER 9

Another weekend had rolled through the lounge. The weeks seemed to just be coming and going at an accelerated rate back in those days. It seemed like we were just locked into the previous weekend and then another weekend was already upon us, but I wasn't complaining though. The faster time went, the faster I got another paycheck. It was just more money hitting the bank for me. Honestly, I needed to replace some of the money I had been spending anyway. We all have things we want and there is always something to spend money on.

I was getting larger and larger tips at the lounge for providing my counseling services. I never was able to quit offering advice to people who needed it, even though Mrs. Kline told me to put an end to it. The money I was making was just too good to pass up. It felt like I wasn't doing anything wrong because the counseling I did on the side never interfered with my ability to bartend and manage the lounge. Besides, what I was doing was not premeditated. All I would do is serve drinks and set up shop as I always did. The next thing I knew, a customer would come in for drinks and ask me for advice on any given topic. I had to do my job and be cordial with the customers, so I entertained their questions. I couldn't just ignore them when they talked to me. I would be insulting the patrons if I did that. Not to mention, I didn't solicit them to come to the lounge for the purpose of counseling them. Additionally, I didn't ask them to pay me for advice they received. We all know that people hand over tips based on how they feel the service is. In some instances, people give modest tips and in other instances they give generous tips. Either way, I didn't have control over what they gave. All I did is accept whatever amount they offered. It was almost like I was addicted to the money. I don't think I could have stopped receiving the money even if I tried.

A guy was in there one night talking to me about a situation his sister was going through. He wanted some advice on what to tell her to do. The gentlemen and I spoke on the subject for quite some time. He was pleased with the information I gave him, so he wrote me a personal check for helping him. I knew the payment was excessive, but it was totally his decision. I didn't have a problem with it.

Unfortunately for me, Mrs. Kline did. She saw the guy hand me the check and also observed me put it in my pocket. She knew there was something shaky about me putting a check in my pocket because we didn't accept checks at the lounge. Mrs. Kline was always a sharp cookie, so she put two and two together and realized that I was still being compensated for giving advice. I hoped she wouldn't say anything to me about it because we had customers in the lounge. I figured if she waited until later that I would have a reason as to why I took the check. Too bad for me, Mrs. Kline decided not to wait to approach me.

"Damn, I know you were shitting bricks when she came over to you! Hell, I know I would have been. I mean, you loved the lounge and really could have lost your job after all the hours you spent putting into making it a success. In the Mix was your life back then. Shoot, it still is now," Sheena orates.

I reply, "Sheena, you know I don't shit bricks. I handle my business accordingly. The rule is to never panic. You know that. After all we've been through, you of all people should know that I don't fret... I cope and conquer."

"Yeah, you're right. Well, what happened when she approached you?" Sheena asks.

Mrs. Kline asked, "Sage, what's going on here? Is there something going on over here that

I need to be made abreast of?"

"Nothing much is going on Mrs. Kline. All is well... just taking care of the customers like normal," I answered.

"Yeah, it surely looks like you're taking care of the customers. Actually, it looks like you're taking care of them almost too well," Mrs. Kline stated angrily.

I knew what Mrs. Kline was talking about, but I wasn't going to mention exactly what I did if she didn't. I tried to downplay the situation. I told Mrs. Kline that I was delivering on the A-plus customer service that the lounge was known for. I was hoping that my charm would get me out of this situation, but it didn't.

Mrs. Kline stated, "I appreciate your dedication to premium customer service because we have to have it, but we still can't charge for it. Now, I may be wrong, but it looked like you just put a check in your pocket. Furthermore, it looked like you are accepting payment for something outside of lounge business."

I answered, "Yes, it is true. I did accept money for business not related to the lounge. The gentleman who just walked away gave me money for some advice I gave him, but I did not ask him for it nor did I ask him to come here for the purpose of receiving advice."

"Sage, we've been down this street before. You're fully aware of how I am against such actions. It does not matter Sage. You were given specific instructions about not doing any side business here at the lounge," Mrs. Kline explained.

"Yes, you gave specific instructions, but I did not intentionally defy you. It kinda just happened, but it doesn't matter anyway," I said.

"It does matter. This is very serious and you take it rather lightly," she told me. "You need to follow the rules that I set forth for this establishment!"

"I don't have to answer to you! What the hell are you gonna do to me?" I asked.

"I can't believe you would speak to me in such a fashion. I have been very nice to you over the years. I have no choice, but to terminate your employment effective immediately. Give me your keys now and vacate the premises. You will be afforded the opportunity at a later date to retrieve your belongings," Mrs. Kline uttered violently.

I responded with a deceitful chuckle, "You're firing me?! You're firing me?!"

Mrs. Kline answered, "Sorry, but it has to be this way. Insubordination will not be tolerated by you or any other employee here. Sage, you're a special person who really knows how to connect with masses of people, but you have to go."

"You can't fire me!" I quickly replied.

She remarked coldly, "The last time I checked, I have the power to do whatever I want here. You are fired!"

"You can't fire me. I own this place!" I said.

Mrs. Kline stated sternly, "I know you've run this place for a while now and you own what I've gifted you, but Sage, the three percent ownership I gave you is not enough to give you say over me. I am the majority owner. On top of that, your partial ownership is only valid while you are employed here. I have fired you, so your three percent comes right back to me. Did you not read what you signed? These items are clearly detailed in our contract."

"It is funny how you mentioned the last time you checked. When is the last time you checked your standings in regards to the lounge? Are you currently the majority owner?" I asked.

"Of course, I am," she answered. "Sage, I don't have to prove anything to you. Your employment here is no longer."

I voiced, "Actually, you are not the majority holder anymore. You currently only own 47 percent of In the Mix."

"Yes, this is true, but it is still controlling interest of the lounge. My ex-husband's percentage is still second to me," Mrs. Kline quoted quoted.

When Mr. and Mrs. Kline got their divorce a while ago the judge granted Mrs. Kline the controlling percentage. Mr. Kline was a bit of a hot head, so the judge punished him by giving him a minority stake in the lounge. This was also a way for Mr. Kline to not pay spousal support. He agreed to them not selling the lounge before the divorce as a compromise. Mrs. Kline was awarded fifty percent, Mr. Kline was awarded forty-six percent, and Jasmine was given four percent.

"No, your 47 percent is not the majority," I replied.

"Well, you're totally correct. Since you are fired, my interest goes right back to fifty percent," Mrs. Kline reported.

"Again, Mrs. Kline you can't fire me and you do not have my three percent ownership. I am the majority owner. I own 53 percent of the lounge's interest," I informed her.

"Wait, wait Baby. That doesn't make any sense. I know you said that Mrs. Kline gave you a few shares and you bought Jasmine out of her shares, but that's only seven percent of In the Mix," Sheena articulates.

"That's right, but I'll finish the story if you let me," I word.

"I'm sorry I keep cutting you off, but this is crazy. I wanna know what happened. Okay, go ahead. I won't cut you off anymore," says Sheena.

Mrs. Kline screamed, "That is impossible. That means that you have my ex-husband's and daughter's share. I know my ex is a greedy old fool and would sell out, but he wouldn't sell it to you. And there's no way in hell Jasmine did!

I decided to go get the paperwork that showed what I was saying was, in fact, the truth.

By then, the entire lounge was looking in amazement.

One dude even screamed, "Takeover!"

When I came back from the office, I let Mrs. Kline read over the contracts.

"I don't believe it. This is unreal and blasphemous. I will let my lawyer review this information to make sure it's certified," Mrs. Kline quoted stated.

"Do whatever you want, but these are all legitimate business moves. I have not a worry in the world. Just so you know, you are fired," I said to Mrs. Kline. "I figure that it's only right that I return the favor that you were going to extend to me."

Mrs. Kline began to stutter her words. She was clearly shaken by the news that was before her. I wish I could have delivered the news to her differently, but I couldn't wait any longer. It was time to let her know what had transpired. It was time for her to go home and enjoy retirement.

She stuttered, "Ho... how...wh... why?"

"You ask why? The answer is simple. I made this place the success it is. When I started here, this place was on the verge of closing its doors. People come here to see me and to seek my advice. Without me, this place is nothing. Without me, you are nothing. That three percent you gave me was nothing. It was an insult. I am worth more than three percent of this place. In addition, we need to expand while the time is right. You didn't want to, so I had to make a move. You are weak and I am strong. Survival of the fittest. When I expand In the Mix to other locations, the bread is gonna double or triple," I explained.

"So, this is just simply about money? Sage, you would cut me so deeply for money? Didn't you say I was like a mother to you?" Mrs. Kline asked.

"You clearly don't understand me. I am done answering questions, but there is nothing simple about what I have done. A lot of planning went into this. I have been scheming on owning this place for a very long time," I explained.

Sheena jumps in and asks, "For years? How did you make it work though?"

"Check this shit out Babe," I voice.

I remember back to the day I went for my initial interview at the lounge. Even before I walked inside to inquire about the job, I saw Mr. and Mrs. Kline arguing. During the interview, the phone to the lounge was ringing off the hook. Next, her cell phone started blowing up too. She answered the phone as I was walking through the lobby area. She argued with who turned out to be Mr. Kline on the phone. At the point when I knew there was discontent in the infrastructure of the organization, I knew it could be infiltrated. I didn't know how, but it came together perfectly. The club allowed me to make many friends and knowledgeable business connects. I knew I would have to use them as pawns to make my plan come to fruition. I had to help as many people as I could to gain support for my takeover. Each person played a valuable part. I knew that I had to get money saved up if I was going to own In the Mix one day. The three main people I needed to swindle were Mr. and Mrs. Kline and their daughter Jasmine. Those three together owned the entire stake of the lounge.

CHAPTER 10

The first time I talked to Jasmine in great detail I knew how I had to play her. She was used to getting a lot of attention from dudes, so I knew flattery wouldn't work on her. She also wasn't driven by people who flashed money at her. It actually turned her away from people. The way to get her where I wanted her to be was through time and patience. I had to convince her that I wasn't like those guys who constantly approached her. She confided her deepest secrets to me. Since she was used to men always trying to approach her, I knew I had to do the opposite. She was beautiful, had a very warm personality, and her body seemed to be designed by a sculptor. I wanted her immensely.

The first time I fucked her was the best experience ever until I met you. I used to wish that we met under different circumstances. Our first sexual encounter was intense and very sensual. One early morning, she stopped by the lounge while I was making some breakfast. We ate and talked about many different things. Before long, Jasmine complained about her back being sore from a new workout she started. She asked me to massage her back for her. Of course, I granted her request without seeming too thirsty.

We went in my room at the lounge, so I could massage her back. She lied on my bed while I massaged her back through her sweater dress. She eventually took her sweater dress off, so I could use some oil to get the job done properly. She also complained she couldn't feel my hands through the thick cloth of her dress. The only thing covering her body were her red lace bra and panties. I unlatched her bra in the back so I could massage her back without obstruction. As I stroked her back, she began to moan in a very seductive manner. The moans were very arousing and made me hard as hell. During the massage, Jasmine noticed I was hard and asked me why it was like that. I told her how I always thought she was attractive and how with her being topless aroused me.

Jasmine mentioned, "That must be painful with it being blocked by your pants like that."

"It is very uncomfortable," I said. "He needs room, but I didn't want to be too forward."

"Let him out. It's just you and me in here. Relax," she stated.

I did as she requested and unbuttoned my pants. I knew where this was going, but I had to play it like it was all her doing. While I was massaging her back, my dick was poking out of the opening in my boxer shorts. It just happened to be very close to her face and she gave it a kiss and started laughing.

"Yo, ya lips are soft as hell! I love the way that felt," I told her. "If you do that again, I'm sure to buss a crazy one."

Jasmine grabbed my dick with both hands and started sucking and licking it. It felt so good that all I could do was grab her tits and go with the flow. I couldn't even talk. I played with her nipples until they were standing at attention and then I picked her up off the bed. We kissed so long and passionately that I almost came on her stomach. She pulled my pants down to my ankles with her feet. When my pants and underwear hit the floor, she pressed her foot down on them allowing me to step out of them without reaching down myself to do it. The flow of our bodies was a pure continuous motion.

I stopped kissing Jasmine and licked her down past her nipples until I reached her panties. I couldn't resist pulling her thong to the side and sticking my tongue in her sweet spot. That wasn't enough because I couldn't eat it the way I wanted, so I pulled her thong off, laid her on the bed, and told her to sit on my face. Her pussy was so wet that I almost drowned. After that, she rode me reverse cowgirl until she went into deep convulsions as she came on my dick.

"It's my turn now. Let me hit it from the back," I told her.

She bent over at the edge of the bed and I inserted my shaft into her tight and wet kitty cat. As I stroked her from behind, she pushed back on my meat, so she could feel the full thrust of my dick. Jasmine was extremely flexible because she lifted both legs up and wrapped them behind me. She was partially airborne while my meat massaged her pouch of pleasure doggy style. We found ourselves fucking in the wheelbarrow position and it was totally spontaneous. The nut I experienced was very intense. I eventually fell to the floor and she landed on top of me. We rested on the floor breathing hard and our hearts were pounding out of our chests.

Every time Jasmine and I got it in, it was just like that. It was always a time to remember. I hated to see her go, but she had to be gone for me to get ownership of the lounge. It hurt me to get her the job overseas, but I knew she wouldn't pass it up. The lady Virginia, who offered Jasmine the job overseas, was related to a customer at the lounge who owed me a favor. Jasmine didn't know that I sent the lady her portfolio. One day Jasmine asked me to help her with updating her résumé and I obliged. Unbeknownst to Jasmine, I made a copy of it and sent it to Virginia.

I knew Jasmine was too independent to let me pay for her move. I played her because I knew her character traits so well. All I did was make it seem like she was in control of the situation and that it wasn't a handout. She made a "Declaration" of what she wanted, so I knew what angle to play. She fell for it. I got her interest in the lounge for close to nothing and she will never get it back. She never did check the paperwork she signed when turning her percentage over to me. That's her bad, not mine. We all have to do what we have to do out here to get what we want. If I didn't do it to her, she might have done it to me. It's either get or be gotten. I chose not to be the victim.

Mr. Kline was the easiest to manipulate of the Kline family members. Mr. Kline was not as difficult to read as Jasmine because he was clear about wanting to get out of the nightclub ownership business. I also knew he wouldn't let me harm Mrs. Kline or Jasmine, so I couldn't buy him out of his ownership. All I had to do was to get someone to offer him something to possibly invest in that was better than the lounge. He jumped at the first mentioning of it. I knew Carol had ample money to make investments with since she got all of that money from her husband in their divorce settlement. I was partly responsible for it because I introduced her to my lawyer James, who took her case for free when she had nothing. She always felt like she was indebted to me for helping her through her divorce. I was her shoulder to cry on during her divorce. I also was her sex buddy. She felt like cheating with me helped her get even with her husband who had cheated on her several times. She would feel better about things after I made her cum a few times. I would fuck her all over the lounge when it closed. She was a real freak to say the least.

Since Mr. Kline was so routine in coming to the lounge for his money, I knew when to tell Carol to come through. She, at my request, staged a fake conversation to get Mr. Kline interested. Before long, he sold his interest in the lounge to her for dirt cheap. It was a simple "Seduction" that lead to his demise. I had been laying the wood to Carol for quite some time, so she was in my pocket. I pulled strings with her like she was a puppet. One night after I had sex with her, we had a little pillow talk. I told her to come to the lounge at the end of the month, and to wear something that would catch Mr. Kline's eye. Eventually, she was supposed to make him talk business. She played the role to perfection. That's how I acquired Mr. Kline's percentage. I didn't pay a dime for it. The plan was for Mr. Kline to sell his share to Carol and then she would sign it over to me. Carol did exactly that. Between money and the hope of a new investment, Mr. Kline was an easy mark. All Carol wanted me to do was keep fucking her.

The money meant nothing to her because she was wealthy.

Getting Mrs. Kline to fall was extremely time consuming and difficult. I didn't know how I would be able to get her to be vulnerable. I knew her vulnerability rested in her trusting nature, but that still didn't translate into ownership for me. I knew that I would have to "Exploit" that somehow. The meeting I had last Halloween in my office was when I put the plan in motion to turn her. During that meeting, I told a buddy of mine who was well versed in expansions to approach her about another location. He also told Mrs. Kline that I was a valuable part of the success of the lounge. Additionally, I had him tell Mrs. Kline that it would be in the best interest of the lounge to make me a partner to some degree. He sold her a dream very easily.

The next day she met with me about expanding. I asked for a small percentage of ownership because I knew she could spare it and still maintain her majority ownership. I knew if I asked the right way, she would be for it. I "Misdirected" her attention when told her I wanted to look at the lounge's expenses to save money. What I was really doing was checking to see how much money was paid to her, Jasmine, and Mr. Kline and to ensure there weren't any other expenses that I didn't know about. I knew she was paid from the lounge's profits each month, so figuring out the percentages of ownership was easy. I figured the judge gave her a percentage that was close to what Mr. Kline had. Once I saw the percentages, I knew the lounge would be mine.

"I'm sure Mrs. Kline was totally disgusted with you," Sheena blurts out.

"You can only imagine! Let me tell you the rest!" I reply.

"Sage, you are full of shit! You are a hypocrite at its finest. Your face probably appears next to the word in the dictionary," screamed Mrs. Kline.

I asked, "How do you figure?

"Since you started here, you've always talked down about how guys use women for sex and how you were bigger than that. You are the same low life you claim to despise," she told.

"Well, according to what I said about those guys is right. I don't see how they use women for sexual exploits. That's a waste of time. I did not do that. I used women's weaknesses not for sex, but for financial gain. It just so happened that I got to get my rocks off in the process. I won," I explained.

"Since I fired you, I get my three percent back. Per our deal, once your employment is terminated, you don't have the three percent. So, it is not as clear cut as you make it," she shot back.

"I see where you are going with this, but it's not going to work. According to the employee handbook, any person who receives monthly payouts from the profits of the lounge is an employee. Even though you attempted to fire me, I am still employed here because I receive monthly payouts from Jasmine's and Mr. Kline's percentage in the lounge," I replied. "You simply don't have the power to fire me, so I'm still employed here and that means I still own your three percent.

"I see, I see. I will make things difficult with what I still own. You can be certain of that," she stated. "I've put decades of my life into this place. I hope you don't think that I'm just gonna hand it over to you."

"This is a hostile takeover. You will be bought out of your percentage of the lounge very soon and will no longer have any affiliation with with it. It was a great run and I appreciate the opportunity, but I have to take my shot at the big leagues. I gotta get mine," I said bluntly.

She replied, "You'll get yours! You will definitely get yours! But those who are self-seeking, who reject the truth and follow evil, there will be wrath and anger."

Mrs. Kline stormed out and I retreated to my office. A few employees didn't like what they saw unfold, so they exited with Mrs. Kline. However, I wasn't surprised. It only made sense that some employees left with her because she hired many of them. I was directly responsible for handpicking several of the staff members and they were the ones who stayed with me. I took care of the ones who remained loyal to me through the change of ownership at the lounge. Many of them still work at the lounge today.

Sheena speaks slightly shocked, "Wow! Sage, all I can say is wow! I can't believe that you took that lady's lounge. It sounds like she was very good to you from the very start and you cut her deeply. I'm surprised that she didn't try to kill you herself as soon as it all went down. Hell, I know I woulda tried to kill you. You know I am not the one for the bullshit. You see how I burned your lounge down when you tried my life with that Ilesha fucking Kevin shit you concocted."

"I know it wasn't my finest moment, but it was one of my moments and I own it. I'm not regretful of any of it. I felt like it was the best move to get me where I wanted to be, so I played the cards that were dealt to me and I won the game," I orate. "The only thing about it all is that it resulted in a few attempts on your life. I definitely could have done without all of that."

Sheena articulates emphatically, "This is some crazy shit you pulled off! I know there's more to the story. Tell me more! Tell me more!"

CHAPTER 11

Things were finally getting back to normal for me at the lounge. It had been a couple of months since I ousted Mrs. Kline and the rest of her family completely from In the Mix. Those first two months were a Hell storm. Although, I knew they would be tough, I didn't expect it to go the way it went. I went from a partial control situation to completely running the show. Running the show all by myself was not a problem for me because I embraced it. I took it as a challenge. The major complication I had over the last two months stemmed from Mrs. Kline mostly. She would call constantly for different reasons. She called for an explanation as to why I did what I did. Then she would call to see if she could pick up her belongings. Majority of the time, she called to curse me out and swear revenge. I wasn't worried about her because she was harmless in my opinion. On many occasions her lawyer called to threaten me about going to court and suing if I didn't make things right for Mrs. Kline. I really loathed him calling me, but guess it was to be expected. The best part about her wanting to sue me was that I knew she had no basis for a lawsuit. People are ousted out of positions all the time in companies, so what I did to her was nothing new. Besides, my lawyer James, told me numerous times that I had nothing to worry about because I conducted all of the business by the book.

Mr. Kline had also been calling me. He felt I was wrong for what I did. He told me one day that I should restore ownership to Mrs. Kline because she loved the place and deserved better than how I did her. She made money off of my hostile takeover. She was in better shape after what I did than she would have ever been. Mr. Kline was only advocating for Mrs. Kline because he was broke. The "potential investment" Carol had for him fell through at the last minute. In all actuality there was no deal for him. It was all a farce that I concocted to get him to sell his portion of the lounge. I used a simple "Misdirection" on him and he was all in. I had Carol give him fifty percent of his money back and we split the rest. He was extremely angry about his deal not going through and felt like I played him too. He would often come in the lounge and stare me down, but wouldn't say anything. He was a bitter and foolish old man. I didn't care about him and his struggles though. The world is a jungle and it's survival of the fittest.

Of course, Jasmine wanted my head on a platter. She sent many emails and texts begging me to fix what I messed up. There was no way that I was giving the lounge back. However, I did feel badly about Jasmine and me not speaking because we were genuinely cool. She even flew back from Europe when her mom told her what transpired to try to convince me to do the right thing. As you can imagine, that was a monumentally heated conversation. At that time, she was the only one who meant anything to me and we were at odds. I loved everything about her, but I loved myself more. I hoped that one day we would be able to reconcile matters, although I was not confident of that ever happening.

Even with all of that drama going on, things were great. I had many enemies formed from the takeover, but I had a lot more money. I stalled on starting In the Mix 2 down in Miami as planned, but wasn't totally off the table. I would've needed to be in two places at once and I wasn't willing to spread myself thin. There's no way I would have been able to finish college if I opened another lounge.

Sheena speaks, "I feel you on finishing college, but you could've made a ton more money by opening a club in Miami. That's like one of the best party cities in the country!"

"Trust me, I know. You don't have to tell me twice. Honestly, I felt like graduating college was something I had to do for myself and my family. You know most of my fam didn't even attend college," I reply sincerely.

Sheena comments, "I totally feel where you're coming from. It's good that you finished what you started and didn't let the money knock you off your square."

"It was a proud moment getting my degree from the real HU! It was worth sticking around for," I tell.

Sheena responds, "I know that's right. You KNOW!"

Sheena and I both chuckle at her response.

"Baby, you were there, so you know how it was. There's nothing quite like it," I shoot back.

Sheena verbalizes, "I agree. Nothing like Howard and there's nothing like being shot. Tell me what happened the day you got shot."

"Okay, it was crazy as hell!" I say.

I wanted to make sure I got some paperwork processed and mailed out, so I went to the lounge early in the morning when nobody was there. I walked into my office and clicked the light switch, but the light didn't come on, so I walked to my desk to turn on my lamp. I sat at my desk and began processing paperwork and ordering supplies. A while later, I heard a noise that clearly came from inside the lounge. I reached in my briefcase and grabbed my gun. Next thing I knew, it there was a man standing in my office. I could see he had a shiny pistol aimed at me.

I asked, "What are you planning to do with that?"

The next thing I heard was the thunder of gunshots. I knew I was hit because I felt an intense burning sensation in my chest. The impact of the shot flipped me out of my chair. I was on the floor bleeding profusely.

"Babe, get the hell outta here! You gotta be fuckin kidding me! I know you were scared as hell," Sheena exclaims.

"Yeah, that's the way it went and it was crazy, but I wasn't scared. I just remember thinking that being afraid or panicking wouldn't help me get out of the situation alive," I utter.

Sheena comments, "Ain't no way in hell that I wouldn't have been screaming, crying, and praying."

I chuckle and remark, "You say that you would've been tripping if it were you in that situation, but you've deftly handled yourself in adverse situations."

"I guess you're right. Hell, I've dodged a few hairy situations in my lifetime to say the least. I ain't gonna lie though…I was scared as hell in all of those moments," Sheena admits.

I start laughing hard and Sheena approaches me. She slaps my arm and pinches me for being so amused at her fright. I curl up in a ball and absorb her playful hits and pinches. Eventually, I reach out and pull Sheena to me and hug her. She playfully pulls away.

"So, the shooter just ran off after he shot you?" Sheena asks.

I answer, "Hell no! When I was on the floor bleeding, I got lucky."

"What happened? Did the guy leave?" Sheena asks.

I answer, "No, he started shooting at me while I was on the floor."

"Sage, I don't see how that's luck!" Sheena says as she cuts me off.

"If you would listen, you'd get the info before you ask the question. I got lucky in two ways. One was the guy missed every time he shot after that. Secondly, when I fell to the floor, so did my gun. Him shooting at me gave me time to get my hand on it and shoot back as he was approaching me," I narrate.

"I am so glad you were able to get to it. I hope you were able to shoot that bastard a couple of times," Sheena words.

I answer, "I don't think I hit him because the guy ran off immediately and wasn't moving like he was hit. Plus, the cops never found any blood other than mine in my office."

"Damn, that would've been good if you would've shot him dead in the office. We might have been able to dodge all of this drama,"

Sheena offers.

"Might have, is right. The cops figured it was an inside job from someone who had intimate knowledge of the lounge. They were intent on causing me harm, so clearly the person wasn't gonna stop until I put an end to the threat," I speak.

"Speaking of inside job. You never said who this mystery man was," Sheena chimes in.

"Damn, my bad Honey! I almost forgot to mention it. The mystery man is definitely an insider. He is Mr. and Mrs. Kline's godson. He was around the lounge off and on over the years. He was a street dude, so it didn't surprise me that he would seek revenge on me. I think once the depression hit Mrs. Kline her godson blamed me and that's when he tried to kill me and then tried to kill you to make me suffer," I explain.

"Well, I'm glad he didn't kill you or me. And no matter what you say, I know getting shot that day was traumatic for you. Being shot is nothing to sneeze at. You know I know," Sheena says as she smiles.

"Oh yeah, I'm glad we got through it. I know you know. Basically, that's what happened back in the day that lead to all of the drama we've been going through lately. It's over now and we can enjoy our lives together peacefully," I orate.

"Yass, I like the sound of that! Peace is something that we've been without for a while now," Sheena tells as she rests her head on my shoulder.

"I'm glad all of that is behind us and I'm just looking forward to being your husband and raising our children," I say as I kiss her on the forehead.

LOVE THIS BOOK AND WANT MORE?

VISIT RYANHODGEBOOKS.COM

MORE BOOKS BY RYAN

The Deception Series:
> *Web of Deception**
> *Wrath of Deception**
> *Will of Deception**
> *Woes of Deception**
> *Rape by Deception***

Historical Science Fiction:
> *Reversed World Power*
Urban Fiction
> *Black Boy Lost, Black Girl Adrift*
Psychological Thriller
> *Deadly Encounter*

*Adult romance
**Suspense Thriller. Spin-off of other novels in series

www.ingramcontent.com/pod-product-compliance
Lightning Source LLC
Chambersburg PA
CBHW071914220626
47052CB00002B/342